I0587437

Within the Range of Reanimation

William H. Nelson

Infinite Worlds Publishing
Within the Range of Reanimation
Copyright © 2019 William H. Nelson
All rights reserved.

EMERGING
INK SOLUTIONS
Kara Scrivener, Editor
www.emergingink.com

Without limiting the rights under copyright reserved above, no part of this publication may be reproduced, stored in or introduced into a retrieval system, or transmitted in any form or by any means (electronic, mechanical, photocopying, recording, or otherwise), without the prior written permission of both the copyright owner and the above publisher of this book.

This is a work of fiction. Names, characters, places, and incidents either are the product of the author's imagination or are used fictitiously. Any resemblance to actual person, living or dead, event, or locales is entirely coincidental.

Other Works by William H. Nelson

NATHROTEP

Acknowledgements

First and foremost, I would like to thank Lisa Paschke. Without her ongoing love and support my stories would most likely never see the light of day. I'd also like to thank my editor Kara Scrivener for all of her hard work and dedication during the revision process.

Additional thanks go out to T.J. Tranchell who did preliminary edits, and to my beta readers, Vaughn Rohrdanz, Jocelyn DeVore, Jake DeVore, Guy Fulton, Maryland Aviuk Panigeo, and Ronald Qiilu Panigeo. Maryland and Ron were also my language consultants; without them this novella would not have been complete. Their tireless efforts in helping me to obtain the correct translation of Iñupiaq dialect was greatly appreciated.

And to my friends and fellow 'Lost Cause' band-mates from Alaska, Michael Ophiem, George Gillis, and Michael Tunohun, I send much gratitude for allowing me to use variations of their last names for the main characters. Thanks guys!

And a very special thanks goes out to Alex Evans. I'd only met him a couple of times at local book signings, but he sent me an unsolicited letter of appreciation at a time when I was seriously considering giving up on writing altogether. It was only after receiving this unexpected message of support that I was able to continue on and write the book that you hold in your hands here today.

And of course, I'd also like to thank all of my friends, family members, and everyone else who has taken the time to read my weird and wondrous works of Lovecraftian fiction throughout the years. Without you, I would never have made it this far. Thank you all so very much!

-1-

"Qaqisailaq..."

I glanced up from the carcass, surprised by his softly spoken observation. Tunuhun was a man of very few words, and when he did choose to communicate, it was only in our native tongue. I shifted around on my knees and then edged forward to peer down at the animal's cranium. The grizzly bear was well over ten feet in length, a large specimen with paws the size of dinner plates. Its broken and battered body lay on the hillside as if it had been dropped from a considerable height. Unbuttoning the top of my parka in the unseasonably warm air, I studied the head of the great beast. Tunuhun was right.

The brains *were* missing.

Just like the other animals we'd stumbled across in the last few hours, the skull had been punctured with numerous, equally spaced holes. There was almost no blood.

Leaning back, I lifted my eyes to scan the trees towering above us. Breaks in the branches showed where the animal had fallen through. It was an unsettling sight, and my hand crept over the rocky soil to grab hold of my rifle. The approaching

1

twilight was drawing long shadows across the land now and I suddenly felt naked without it. This place was taking its toll on me, taking its toll on all of us.

As if my thoughts had summoned him, Opeim appeared at the foot of the trail. His eyes took in everything as he held his firearm with a deceptive nonchalance that seemed almost lackadaisical. Yet his relaxed posture didn't fool me for a second; I knew the man was ready to fire that weapon at a moment's notice and with pinpoint accuracy. It was one of the reasons I'd chosen him for this expedition.

"Let's get the hell out of here," he whispered in a strained voice. "We should go back now. Back to the village! We've seen enough. This is bad, Gillam – we should *not* be here!"

In a way, I knew he was right, but that still didn't make it a viable option. Night was falling and we were far from the small community to which we belonged. Too far to make it back in one evening. I glanced around, thinking things through.

"The elders need to know what's happening to the animals," I said after a moment. "They need to know what this immense, smoking mountain is that's suddenly appeared. We can't go back until we find out more."

"This is bullshit!" Opeim exclaimed, putting his back against a tree while his eyes continued to search our surroundings in the failing light.

With a fluid ease, Tunuhun stood and retrieved his weapon from where he'd leaned it against a weathered stump, staring at me with his usual somber expression. I was in charge here and it was up to me to make the decisions.

Whether they liked them or not.

I stood, pulling the rifle up with me. The air was still and silent, the odor of the bear carcass a sharp, pungent attack on my senses. I gazed around at the trees clustered across the hillside. We were on a rumpled slope that led up to a mountain, a mountain that hadn't been there a few days before. During the earthquake, it had thrust itself up from the frozen ground like the back of a gargantuan whale breaching the surface of the Arctic Sea and then climbing to an even greater height, rivaling the daunting majesty of the surrounding Brooks Range. Its summit now stood wreathed in clouds. Some said they'd witnessed white smoke billowing out from it as it struggled aloft. Many speculated it was a new volcano being born. Even now, I was uncertain of what it could possibly be.

Earlier, as we'd worked our way across one of the huge knuckles of earth and permafrost that had broken upward from its base, we'd also taken note of the enigmatic smoke that had been present for the last couple of days. There was noticeable heat in the air here as well, but it wasn't trees burning just beyond these hills; there'd been no odor, no sparks or flames reflecting across the lead-gray skies. No, this was something else entirely.

Gazing down at the broken thing lying at my feet, I studied the fierce creature that had once been such a powerful presence here in these lands. Whatever it was that was waiting for us at the summit of this inexplicable place, it was nothing good. Of that much I was certain.

I signaled to Opeim and he swallowed his anger, shooting me a look of thinly veiled resentment as he turned and headed back toward our camp, melting away amongst the spruce and alder. Glancing at Tunuhun, I acknowledged his curt nod of acceptance; he understood me well enough. The temperature was dropping fast as night came on and I knew that we'd do better returning to camp for now and then starting fresh in the morning. Earlier Tunuhun had taken point, being the best tracker and the most skilled in forest craft; I had needed his expertise to find us the safest route.

Then the mutilated animals we'd encountered along the way had slowed our progress as we had paused each time to puzzle over our discoveries. It was the reason why we hadn't quite made it to the top of the ridgeline yet. But nothing we'd found thus far had made much sense to any of us. All we really knew was that we had big trouble on our hands, maybe even bigger than we could handle.

Nonetheless, I decided we were well-equipped for it and our stealthy advance had surely given us an edge. Whatever it was that was killing these animals, it couldn't possibly know that we were stalking it. Not yet, at least.

The walk back to camp would go quicker, and therefore be more dangerous. It was why I needed Opeim on point now as he was the safer bet for our continued survival. Tunuhun would bring up the rear in case something chose to follow us. He'd proven in the past that nothing could get by him. I just hoped we'd make it back without him having to prove it once more. Settling the gun into the crook of my arm, I struck out, using the skills I'd learned growing up to pass down the trail in silence like a wraith, Tunuhun fading into the mists behind me.

We'd covered perhaps half a mile before my mind began wandering, thinking back on what had led me into this situation. The elders had wanted us to wait. With the radio out and another group chosen to head toward the larger settlement on the coast for help, they'd wanted everyone left in the village to stick together, to hold tight until we saw what happened next. I had been the only one out of our small community who'd traveled beyond our lands to study. The universities I'd attended had broadened my understanding of the world around us and I'd argued at the time that we didn't have the luxury to wait. In my opinion, we needed to find out what was happening before more trouble came our way.

I'd expected resistance, but the elders had surprised me. After a short, whispered conference, they'd agreed. I was to pick two men and make my way to the ridges that formed the base of this new mountain. There, I was to ascertain why the animals were fleeing in our direction with madness in their eyes, determine what was causing the unseasonable warmth and the peculiar, billowing smoke, and find out just what this unexpected geological event would mean for the continued survival of our entire tribe.

Looking back, it struck me then that there was a reason I'd been selected; my hard-won knowledge and foreign ideas threatened the old ways. In fact, my voice in counsel was an inadvertent stab at their authority and undermined the continuance of all our ancient traditions. The younger members of our settlement often looked up to me now and my innovative approach to problem-solving had begun to influence them. Knowing all of this, there was only one conclusion I could draw from their eager capitulation.

I'd been sent out here to die.

Slowing to a stop along the trail, I turned that idea over in my mind. It was an unsettling realization and troubled me to the very core of my being. Was it really why I'd been sent on this mission, or was I just growing paranoid out here? Squinting up at the gray cloud bank overhead, I estimated our remaining daylight. It would be dark soon and this place was wearing on my nerves. The unexpected seismic activity, the sudden appearance of the mountain, and now the animals we'd found with those surgically precise holes drilled in their skulls – all of these things were becoming more worrisome the longer I considered them.

Just what the hell was going on out here? What was it worth for me to discover the answer to this question? Was I really willing to die in these mountains to find out the truth behind this troubling mystery?

Before I could come to any satisfactory conclusions, a shot rang out from farther down the slope. Cocking my head to one side, I stood listening. But there was nothing more after that except the echo of the gun's report ringing out across the frigid air.

I started forward again, only to feel an iron-firm grip on my shoulder, jerking me to a stop. Glancing back, I found Tunuhun gazing at me, his weather-beaten face serious in the shrouded twilight, his dark eyes boring into mine with a look of mild reproach. Then, lifting his hand, he cupped it next to his mouth and sounded a bird call. A green-winged teal, I think it was. After a long, tension-filled moment, the return signal came back. It was the trill of a red-breasted merganser. Using hand signals, we determined our next course of action and then split up, moving across the hillside while putting some distance between us.

Maneuvering down the slope, we soon converged upon a small bluff that overlooked the base camp. Opeim was kneeling there with his shoulder pressed up against a tree, his Browning .30-06 sighted down and to the right. Crouching next to him, I peered at the encampment, trying to see what he was aiming at. The visibility was poor, but I could tell right away that there was nothing there. Just the fog-shrouded aspens and humped boulders blocking the wind from our campsite.

"What are you shooting at?" I whispered.

"There was something down there," he replied, "something rooting around by our tent. I think there were two of them, but I can't be sure."

"What was it?" I asked, edging up to the lip of the overhang to get a better view. "Was it an animal of some kind?"

He lowered his rifle. His face, when he turned toward me, was strained. "I don't know what the hell it was. Some kind of... kind of creature that I've not seen before. I think... I think I hit one... they ran off into that ravine."

The fact that he wasn't sure of his aim made me grunt in surprise. He never missed. My eyes narrowed as I studied him. He didn't look so good – something had him spooked. I glanced over at Tunuhun who was watching the darkening woods to our left, his rifle hard against one shoulder. He didn't seem concerned, but, then again, he never did. I knew our options were becoming limited. If Opeim had wounded an animal, then it was going to be dangerous, especially if it was a predator. And that ravine led to an enclosed box canyon. We'd scouted it out just this morning before making camp and found that it ended in a jumble of boulders and scree that had rolled down the hillside when the mountain had first struggled aloft. Whatever it was, the element of surprise was now lost to us; that gunshot pinpointed our location to anyone within a mile radius of the campsite.

I studied the area below us again, looking and listening for other signs of intrusion. There was nothing. And the darkness was getting heavier. I glanced back over at Opeim and then laid a hand on his shoulder.

"Let's get down there and build up the fire. Then we'll scout around a bit, make sure that whatever it was isn't going to double-back on us."

"No."

I was surprised by his sudden, flat-out refusal. It was a shock to realize he was well and truly frightened. This man who I'd grown up with, who had sailed on the Arctic Sea to hunt whales in an *umiak* made of seal skins, who had once faced down a charging polar bear and then later laughed about it, this man was now somehow gripped by overwhelming terror. Glancing again at Tunuhun, I noticed that his face was grave as he stared back at us. I was responsible for both these men. I held their lives in my hands and it was a burden that I took very seriously. Nodding to myself, I came to a decision.

"Tunuhun and I will scout around while you keep the fire built up and get our things ready to go. We're getting out of here as soon as there's light enough to travel."

The look of relief he gave me was almost palpable.

Angling around the ridge, we came down into the camp, scanning our surroundings as we progressed. But nothing I could see was an immediate threat. The wall of boulders that protected us from the wind was on the left while the game trail we'd noticed this morning veered off to the right, disappearing into the shallow ravine which paralleled the hillside. Our fire pit was prepared and ready to go, so Tunuhun and I stood guard as Opeim knelt down to kindle it. As the wood caught and the fire flared to life, I saw that all of our gear, which had been stored in our packs before we ascended the hill, was now neatly spread out across the rocky, moss-covered ground. Stranger than that, it was laid out in a loose geometric pattern, all of the items dismantled and placed end-to-end like someone had been trying to determine their function.

Opeim snatched up his rifle, surging erect as he stumbled backward with a look of uncompromising fear scrawled across his sparsely-bearded features. Tunuhun just grunted in mild surprise. Then, in unspoken agreement, we all moved away from the fire, stepping over the items to put our backs to the largest boulder behind the tent. Crouching down, Tunuhun scrutinized the strange design made from our equipment. It looked to me like some type of flowering, star pattern. I had no idea who or what could have made it.

Searching the darkness on the other side of the fire pit, I noted that the wind had picked up, blowing away some of the ground fog as the temperature plummeted. It was growing colder by the minute but the fire was blazing now and it created a small pocket of warmth. It also deadened my night vision – other than the windblown fog, I couldn't see a damn thing out there.

"Could it have been some men that were down here?" I asked, keeping my rifle leveled at the darkness beyond the flames. "Maybe someone from the village that followed us?"

"No," Opeim said. "These things were... they had... My God, Gillam! I know what I saw, but I don't even know how to describe it! The fog was thick, but these things were crouched by our tent. I could see something moving around their heads, like antlers but different, and their backs were knobby and covered in pink skin. I know that sounds crazy, but dammit! I know what I saw! It was getting dark and I was going to come back up the trail to warn you, but then I heard it..."

He paused, his eyes darting back and forth, lips trembling and jaw working as he tried in vain to find words to describe what he'd seen, what he'd heard.

"It wasn't men," he finally choked out. "By god, Gillam, it was *not* men! The sounds that they made, the noises I heard – it was like nothing I've ever heard before. I'm telling you, it wasn't human! I... I was about to come back up to you, and then... and then one of them must have sensed me. It turned and... Oh my God! I shot it! I had to shoot it, Gillam!"

He was babbling. It was a bad sign. I glanced down at Tunuhun and he looked up at me, shaking his head. He had found nothing in the carefully laid out jumble of our belongings. I rotated my index finger in a circle and he gathered himself to begin working his way around the fire, dropping into a crouch every so often and taking his time. If Opeim had shot anything, there would be some sign of it, blood or some other type of spoor we could follow. I wasn't looking forward to venturing out into the freezing darkness, but neither could I wait until we were attacked. In my experience, when something was wounded, be it man or beast, it was best to find it before it found you. Whatever jrwas, we had to do something fast. I motioned to Opeim.

"Gather up the gear and get it stowed. We'll need a couple of those lanterns, some flares, and plenty of spare ammo. Separate it out for us before you pack up the rest – we're going to need to move as soon as possible."

-2-

I could see Opeim fighting to control his fear and anger, his face twitching through a gamut of emotions that distorted his features into a parody of his normal expression. He opened his mouth as if to argue, but then closed it as Tunuhun's voice drifted out of the darkness.

"Auk igliguuruq-taqqatigun ikillauruq."

He had found something – and it was not reassuring. Kneeling on the far side of the fire, I saw him studying the bark of a nearby tree. Something glistened there, something wet and shimmering in the shifting firelight. He was correct; blood had indeed flowed through the veins of something and now that something, or someone, was wounded, probably angry, and possibly waiting just beyond our range of Vision. I didn't know what we were going to find out in the icy darkness of that dead-end ravine, but I did know that we'd better take care of it and then get the hell out of this godforsaken place as fast as possible. With that in mind, I motioned to Opeim to hurry with the gear.

We wound up with two powerful belt lanterns, an LED blackout torch, six hand flares, a pocket-sized med kit, and extra shells for both rifles. Opeim was on edge and clearly unhappy, but he kept himself busy by gathering equipment while Tunuhun examined the ground around the base of the tree. Lost in thought, I stood guard over them both.

My plan was to make a quick foray to the end of the ravine and back. Afterward, we would keep the fire blazing through the rest of the night while waiting for daybreak. It was the best plan I could come up with under the circumstances and I figured that we'd better get it done while we still had the chance.

It was much colder now. The temperature was still dropping as the wind fragmented the fog into shadowy wisps of vapor that floated through the trees like sullen spirits. Ice crystals sparkled in the air as well and our breath appeared in plumes that swirled around our heads as we made ready to depart. I judged that our supply of firewood was adequate and I didn't think we'd run out during the night. It was time to go.

Moving around the fire, I knelt and aimed my flashlight at the smear of fluids splattered across the tree trunk. The dark liquid was already partially crystallized from the cold, yet as I peered at it, I noted how thick and uncoagulated it appeared, how it was more purplish in coloration than red. It seemed to shift in the artificial light, an oily, prismatic glimmer that gave off an unsettling spectrum of colors. The more I studied it, the more uneasy I became. What kind of animal – or man, for that matter – had blood that reacted this way?

When I turned my head to stare at it from the corner of my eye, it oozed with a movement all its own, like it was made up of uneasily joined particles seething at the molecular level. I glanced over at Tunuhun to find him staring out into the night, his rifle held ready in his large, capable hands. Down the trail off toward the ravine, the wind moaned as it picked up speed. To see his steadiness in the face of such bizarre circumstances was reassuring. The man was unshakable. Turning to glance back over my shoulder, I spoke to Opeim.

"We're going to go have a look around. Keep the fire built up and stay alert. As soon as we return, I'll help you get the rest of the gear packed up and then we'll sleep in shifts, two men guarding and one man resting. No sense in taking any chances."

I had meant it to sound reassuring, but he returned my gaze with the flat, dead eyes of a halibut. I didn't like the expression that now clung to his sallow face. Moving back around the fire, I grasped his shoulder. "Look, we're heavily armed, Tunuhun is the best tracker in the entire village, and that trail leads to a dead end. We won't be gone long. Whatever it is that you shot, we'll make sure it's no longer a threat and then come right back. They couldn't have gotten far, not if you've wounded one of them. I need you to stay sharp and keep the campsite safe for us – can you do that?"

He hesitated and I could see his pale features squirming while an internal struggle raged within him. Then, as he mastered his emotions, resolve entered his eyes and I witnessed a visible change come over him as he shook off his fear and uncertainty. Grasping my arm and meeting my gaze with a look of unshakable determination, he nodded his head. Here was the man I knew so well, that I'd grown up with and had always admired for his steadfast abilities. Upon seeing his newfound resolution, a sense of relief washed through me.

Without further discussion, I stepped away, tallying up our resources mentally while debating the advantages of our night vision over the belt lanterns. In the end, I decided it would be better to light up our surroundings and then use the blackout torch to focus our shots if needed. Not only would that make any animals leery of charging us, it would also blind them if they attempted it.

With this in mind, I motioned to Tunuhun and he started forward, keeping low to the trail and stopping every few steps to study the ground. As I proceeded along behind him, our combined lanterns illuminated a wide circle around us, and in this manner, we progressed into the freezing wind, penetrating the darkness with man-made light.

I had to admit to myself that I was beginning to get a bit frightened; it would have been foolish to be otherwise. But our strength of arms and the considerable abilities we shared between us were more than enough to handle whatever we now hunted. At least, that's what I kept telling myself as we moved farther from the fire and deeper into the surrounding twilight.

We had been walking for perhaps 15 minutes following after the traces of blood when I realized the air was growing warmer again. Tunuhun seemed to recognize this as well because he glanced back, signaling for me to stop. Up ahead, there was a bend in the trail marked by a large boulder sitting just off to the right. Switching off his belt lantern, he crept up to this obstruction and then, sliding his shoulder along its rough surface, craned his neck around the edge to peer beyond it. After a moment, he jerked his head back, motioning for me to extinguish my light and then come forward.

With the rifle held in my right hand, I pocketed the blackout torch and then reached down to switch off my lantern. Darkness swallowed us and I was blind for a few seconds as my eyes adjusted to the sudden lack of illumination. Staring through tears made by the stinging wind, I was shocked to discover a purplish glow emanating from the opposite side of the boulder, outlining it in an ethereal nimbus. Silent as a stalking lynx, I crept closer.

As I reached Tunuhun's side, he gestured for me to look around the edge of the obstruction. Putting my back to the cold surface of the stone, I cautiously peeked around it. What I saw went far beyond the realm of all my expectations.

Ahead in the confines of the narrow ravine there now stood a profusion of glowing, crystalline pillars. It was as if the inside of a geode had cracked open and columns of celestite had exploded from it, covering the ground in clusters of geometric splendor. These strange formations saturated the darkness with an uncanny violet radiance as they stood in random groupings around an octagonally-shaped tunnel that burrowed straight down into the hillside. Steam billowed from the interior of this passage and the shaft, lit from within by its own spectral illumination, seemed to lead into the very bowels of hell itself.

When we had scouted this area earlier, there had been nothing here besides a dead-end covered by boulders and scree. Who could have excavated this smooth-sided tunnel, created these crystalline formations? They were definitely not man-made. My mind raced as it tried to make sense of it all and I felt the insidious tendrils of fear growing ever stronger within me. Just what the hell was going on out here?

Before my churning thoughts could formulate any logical answers, an audible reverberation disrupted my silent musings. It was like several sections of wet canvas being slapped together, a soggy, repetitive noise accompanied by a methodical whooshing that made the hairs at the base of my neck stand on end.

As I continued watching the tunnel in bewilderment, shadows formed deep within it and then flowed upward as the sounds increased in volume.

Mixed with the steam and illuminated by the glowing crystals, a swarm of dark shapes flew forth, spiraling up into the night sky. I couldn't see them clearly, but the impression I got was that of a cluster of huge, bat-like entities flying in tight formation as they swirled upward into the cold, arctic night.

Ducking back behind the cover of the boulder's edge, I tried to calm my racing heart. In that moment, a lone thought struggled to the surface of my mind – they were heading straight for our camp!

Without hesitating, I turned to run back the way we'd come. I had to warn Opeim, had to save him from whatever it was that now flew through the heavens like a flock of eldritch nightmares sprung to life from out of a fractured fairytale. But before I'd even taken two steps, Tunuhun grabbed me around the collar and yanked me back, throwing me up against the weather-beaten stone and placing his hand over my gasping mouth to stifle my surprised exclamation.

Gazing at him in wide-eyed disbelief, I noted his impassive expression, the same expression he often wore while we were playing cards together. Releasing my mouth, he placed one hand firmly against my chest and made the signal for danger with the other, indicating the opposite side of the boulder. Fighting down my rising panic, I slid to the edge of the stone and peered around it once more.

Two shadowy figures now stood within the wind-swept darkness. They must have emerged from the tunnel while I was preparing to warn Opeim. The realization hit me then that, had I started back toward our campsite as planned, these creatures would have seen me for sure. Grateful for Tunuhun's intervention, I took a deep, steadying breath, settling my nerves enough to regard what I was seeing with scientific detachment. It helped me to know that Tunuhun was a stalwart presence at my back and after a moment, my heartbeat slowed as I began to study the things with a more level-headed curiosity, taking note of their bizarre characteristics in the eerie twilight.

They stood about five feet tall with strange, oval-shaped heads. But that's where the similarities to anything even remotely human ended. From where we hid in the shadows, I could tell they had multiple sets of limbs, many appearing crustaceous in nature, attached to a long, segmented body. Pink-colored skin ran down their knobby backs and then out along their insect-like abdomens while a prismatic series of lights danced about in the air above their heads. I realized that the flashes of color throbbing across the somewhat lumpy surface of their elongated skulls was caused by dozens of bio-luminescent stalks or tentacles radiating outward from the top of each cranium.

As I continued to gape at them in stupefied wonder, one of them turned to reenter the tunnel while the other pivoted and scuttled straight toward me. Backing away from the edge of the stone, I turned to warn Tunuhun of its imminent arrival.

But found, much to my consternation, that he was no longer there.

The things that flashed through my mind in that moment were hard to reconcile. I was taken aback by his sudden absence and unable to decide how best to proceed. With mounting anxiety, I turned back, watching as the creature came around the edge of the massive boulder. Discovering my presence, its pincers spread wide and it advanced on me with what could only be considered as malicious intent. The closer it got, the better I could make out the complex details of its astounding anatomy, and I was horrified by its utter alienness.

The feelers radiating from the surface of its head were like a sea anemone's tentacles, bio-luminescent and moving independently, while the skull itself resembled a large sponge with many convoluted crevices and fleshy, circular rings. Yet there were no obvious signs of an ocular system or any other organs used for visual acuity. Shaken by the bizarre anomaly of its appearance, all I could do was stare while the smooth portion of its lower jaw pulled apart, revealing multiple sets of wickedly serrated mandibles. From between these ghastly mouth parts came a bundle of long, pink tendrils with small, round clusters of serrated teeth swirling at the tips like rolling, mill-toothed drills. These cilia-like organs were accompanied by an unwholesome buzzing, not unlike a dense swarm of bees preparing to defend its queen. Lacking the willpower to even back away, I stood rooted in place, the rifle forgotten in my trembling hands.

In that moment, silent as an owl, Tunuhun dropped on the creature from above, grasping a handful of the thing's cranial tentacles. Without hesitation, he then wrenched its head back to draw his hunting knife straight across the ridges of its exposed neck cartilage. Falling to the ground in a pile of thrashing arms and legs, they rolled over and over across the windswept tundra before coming to stop in a tangled, shuddering heap.

Extricating himself from the creature's twitching limbs, he rose from the ground in one fluid motion, not even winded by his actions. Glancing upward, I surmised that he must have leapt from the top of the boulder in order to catch his prey unaware. My eyes darted back to him in appreciative awe and I caught him squinting at me as he wiped the long, gore-covered hunting knife along his seal skin leggings. Sheathing the freshly cleaned blade at his waist, he then peered at the shuddering creature, making a shouted observation over the moaning of the arctic wind.

"Tuungaq pigitchuq."

I couldn't agree with him more; the devil *was* bad and I was immensely relieved I hadn't found out just how bad that this particular devil could be. He motioned for me to assist him and together we dragged the thing behind a small stand of trees.

It was lighter than I expected, its knobby, pink flesh now ridged in death and its crustacean-like appendages covered in the familiar purplish fluid we'd been following earlier. At this point, I suddenly remembered Opeim. Tunuhun must have been struck by the same thought, for the look that he turned on me was one of deepening concern.

We had to warn our friend before those flying creatures could discover the campsite.

But just then a series of shots rang out, resounding across the frigid night air, and our eyes met, both knowing that we were already too late.

-3-

With a few hand signals, I sent Tunuhun heading up the hillside to our left. We had lost the element of surprise, so I intended to race down the trail as fast as I could while Tunuhun maneuvered across the wooded slope. My plan was to catch the creatures in a crossfire if we could manage it. It was an old hunter's strategy, and one that had worked well for us in the past. Gripping the rifle tight to my chest in the freezing darkness, I set off at a run toward our camp as Tunuhun melted away amongst the trees.

My night Vision was more than adequate with the belt lantern switched off, and so I increased my pace down the now familiar trail. These creatures, whatever they were, could be killed. We had proven that just moments ago. I only hoped that we'd be able to get to Opeim before they overwhelmed him.

Panting in mild exertion, I soon closed in on the location of the camp, the firelight leaking between the tree trunks casting long shadows around me. Up ahead, I heard another shot split the night air, as well as the flapping of several sets of wings coupled with a high-pitched whistling noise, like steam being driven from a tea kettle. The sound washed over me in disjointed waves as the wind picked it up and sent it spiraling outward. Between the sparse branches, I saw our campsite painted in orange and amber light by the roaring fire. Skidding to a halt at the edge of the woods, I put my shoulder against a large pine and then sighted down the barrel of my rifle.

Opeim stood with his back to the largest boulder behind our tent, the fire in front of him blazing high, its flames licking upward and scattering shadows across the camp. From above, several of the creatures dove at him, their multiple sets of legs highlighted from beneath by the fire's flickering ambience. As I surveyed the scene, trying to pick a target, he fired at one of them and it swerved away, screeching like the emergency brake on a speeding locomotive. On the ground before the fire lay a crumpled, knobby-looking shape. It appeared he had already killed one of the foul things so perhaps we were not too late after all. Without further hesitation, I began to shoot at the other fire-dappled monstrosities still swarming the air above him.

It was strange, but the arctic wind seemed to have no effect on their ability to fly. It was as if the air went right through them, never quite touching their gyrating bodies. As I continued to fire at the creatures, they veered away, heading higher into the starlit sky, and for the briefest of moments, I could see a nimbus surrounding them, a blurred outline which pulled them out of focus to my squinting eyes.

Moving from tree to tree, I slipped closer through the forest, trying to find a better vantage point. It was then that Opeim saw me and tried to make a run for it.

However, as soon as he moved from the protection of the campfire, one of the creatures was upon him, its hideous claws clamping down on his shoulders to haul him, kicking and screaming, into the air. Diving into a shoulder roll, I landed on my back, skidding across the frost-covered clearing while trying to get a bead on his assailant. Unfortunately, the creature was now just a fuzzy shadow in the darkened sky as it carried Opeim off toward the ravine. In frustration, I surged to my feet, but before I could make it back to the shelter of the trees, another of the creatures plummeted down in an attempt to latch onto me.

At this point it was the rifle that saved me. Instinctively, I'd thrown up my arms to ward off its attack and the crab-like pincers that had been meant for my flesh hooked onto the weapon instead. The mass of the thing was almost indescribable. At one moment, it was like being pressed down by hundreds of pounds of weight; in the next, it seemed like I was being pulled upward by a large string of helium balloons. Wrenching back on the rifle, I struggled to regain control, but was dragged across the fire instead and then over to the tumble of boulders beyond it. That's when I got a closer look at the writhing abomination that now towered above me.

This one was different from the others, larger and more powerfully built. Its head, now looming over me, had oversized mandibles with jagged serrations running the length of them, while the top of its skull had the stunning appearance of an exposed brain with dozens of worm-like tentacles sprouting from the creases. These flexible stalks that writhed outward from the central mass were fully segmented and lacked the coloration of the ones we'd seen earlier, trending toward dull reds and yellows.

While trying to wrest the gun from its vice-like grip, I realized I would soon lose this contest of wills. Grasping the weapon with the remainder of my waning strength, I fell backward, putting my weight behind the desperate action and landing across one of the smaller boulders beneath us. But the thing's density suddenly increased again and the air was driven from my lungs as I was crushed under its weight. Struggling to regain my breath, there was nothing I could do as the rifle was torn from my hands and tossed across the fire. From between those horrible mandibles then came masses of spiraling tubules like the ones I'd seen on the smaller creature, yet these were enormous, the tips capped with rotating, three-beveled teeth that reminded me of an oilfield drill. I screamed as they shot toward the top of my head with the obvious intent of boring straight into my skull.

From out of the frozen darkness, Tunuhun suddenly appeared, springing from the top of an adjacent boulder to land on the creature's back, his knife, like a streak of molten silver in the light of the blazing fire, arching toward the thing's exposed brain-like cranium. He must have decided against firing his own rifle for fear of hitting me in the process, but I was glad to see him nonetheless as his blade flashed toward the soft tissues of the creature's convoluted head. But at the last possible moment, bony protuberances like the forelimbs of a praying mantis erupted from beneath the monster's lower jaw. These plates of solid chitin closed over the top of the creature's vulnerable skull with an audible snap and sent Tunuhun's knife skittering off along the hard ridges of its knobby spine.

With a near deafening screech, the thing bucked, neither losing its grip on the front of my parka, nor seeming burdened at all by Tunuhun's weight.

In that brief airborne second, I drew my own knife, angled it up between its gaping jaws and, twisting my head away from the masses of drill-tipped cilia, plunged the blade deep into the cleft of its soft palate. The keening sound that it made then was thunderous and as its full weight came crashing down upon me, I squirmed, trying desperately to pull myself from beneath its flailing appendages.

It was in that exact moment that the earth shrugged beneath me and with a sound like a groaning land-slide, the ground split open to swallow us whole. As we fell into the depths, I struck my head, losing consciousness in a flash of light and shadows.

———◇———

When I came back to my senses, a watery light was filtering into my eyes from far above and my head ached, but I didn't feel queasy or sleepy. Just judging from that, I assumed I was in better shape than could be expected after receiving a blow to the skull. Squinting against the glare, I discovered that we'd fallen into a crack made by the unexpected earthquake during the attack. Shaking my head to clear it, I wondered what had become of Tunuhun.

As I sat up, I caught sight of him. He was cloaked in shadows, sitting with his legs crossed beneath him, his face entirely hidden, his body motionless. But as I gathered myself, he leaned forward into the feeble sunlight. His features were bruised, but otherwise undamaged. It seemed that, other than a few minor injuries, we'd both been lucky.

I glanced to the left and saw a lumpish shape lying closer to the wall of the chamber. We must have landed on top of the creature, breaking our fall. Whatever these things were, at least this one had done us that much of a favor. It was really the only positive thing I could say about this whole misadventure so far.

Crawling over to its mangled body, I studied it in the dim illumination. It was much larger than the ones we'd seen earlier, its hardened carapace bulkier and its multiple legs bulging with twisted musculature and stiff, wiry hairs. While the upper half of its torso was greenish-gray in color, the underside tended more toward flesh tones.

Surveying the rest of it, I saw that the lumpy mass that served as its head still had the extra set of mandible-like forelimbs locked over it. I surmised that this unique form of protection was specific to this variation of the creature. Perhaps it was some breed of soldier. Thinking about it, they did bear a striking resemblance to several insect species familiar to me, as well as sharing similarities with various crustaceous sea life. However, the wings, which were far less bat-like than I had at first imagined, appeared more like the multiple sets found on dragonflies, but non-transparent and fleshier in form. I had no idea how they even lifted off the ground with such an obvious imbalance in weight ratios. Its ability to fly with such mismatched proportions baffled me.

Peering into the thing's mouth, I examined the tendrils of its feeding tubes, now lax in death, noting the peculiar, three-beveled teeth at the tips of each one. The woodland animals we'd found with those surgically precise holes in their skulls were no longer a mystery to me now. These beings had been gorging themselves on brains and they were powerful enough to lift a full-sized grizzly bear from the ground and then kill it while remaining airborne. A wave of dizziness washed over me as I thought about that. The two of us were fortunate indeed to have survived the attack on our camp.

With a grimace of disgust, I reached between the thing's multiple, serrated jaws and wrenched my knife from inside its mouth cavity. The resulting wet suction noise as the blade slid free was accompanied by a gush of purplish fluids that had a smell not unlike that of cloves or cmnamon.

When I turned to share my observations with Tunuhun, he motioned me to silence, gesturing off to his left where the rest of the cave system stretched away into darkness. With a series of hand signals that we'd both known since childhood, he warned me that there was danger nearby. It would seem that we weren't out of the woods yet. Never far from my mind was also the fact that these things, whatever the hell they were, had taken Opeim. Gathering my wits about me, I shifted back into the shadows, studying the rest of our cavernous prison with speculative interest.

The striations on the wall next to me told me that this place was ancient, perhaps even hundreds of thousands of years old. Searching our surroundings, I found that the natural rock was supplemented with sheets of another material I could not readily identify. Broken pieces of it lay strewn across the ground while partial sections of it still stood amongst other undamaged segments farther down the way from us. These upright slabs were all very thin and clustered together in interlocking patterns like the leaves of a geometric puzzle.

Without a sound, I drew myself to my feet and moved closer to the nearest selection of still intact artificial panels. What I found there surprised me.

The slabs were semitransparent and revealed a different shade of orange or red on each separate leaf. Incised into these thin sections were markings and odd shapes. At first, I couldn't tell what they represented, but by standing back a little and peering at them from out of the corner of my eye, I was able to ascertain what they actually were.

Like early Sanskrit or other ancient pictographic languages, the panels, when observed from an odd angle, blended together to display what can only be described as a historical record. It was too foreign for me to piece together, but the section I was puzzling over seemed to portray a struggle of sorts between the creatures that had made this cavern and another race of beings equally unfamiliar to me. Their enemies, for surely that was what they must be as I considered the brutality of the pictographs, were barrel-shaped with angular, starfish-shaped heads. That was all I could really make out with the naked eye as the slabs were obviously meant to be read by beings with a sense of perception far greater than my own. It was a sobering thought which brought me back to our current dilemma.

Tunuhun had ghosted up as I was studying the unusual inscriptions and he now motioned for me to follow as he set off farther into the gloomy darkness. I didn't know where he was heading, but it occurred to me that I'd been unconscious for a while and, in that time, he'd had plenty of opportunity to scout around. I followed him in silence, trusting his instincts to see me safely through the rest of the stygian corridors.

Upon reaching a bend in the tunnel, I discerned a faint, bluish glow emanating from the other side of an open archway situated a couple feet away from us. The cave system, with its many pictographic slabs, split off in several directions from here, but I had no immediate desire to explore any of these other chambers. Time was of the essence now and we needed to find Opeim and get the hell out of this place. That idea was foremost in my thoughts as Tunuhun signaled that I should peer around the edge of the tunnel opening.

As I moved to glance around the corner, I was once again impressed by the construction techniques used in making the frame of the doorway itself. It was another octagonal shape, finely crafted and smooth to the touch. That was all I had time to notice, for on the other side of it was a glowing, blue corridor filled with several of the smaller creatures.

They bustled about, some standing and conversing in their peculiar language, using gestures and the writhing of their colorful head tentacles, while others scuttled to-and-fro on errands I could not even begin to guess at. The hallway curved off to the right, continuing out of our visual range, but there was another octagonal door set in the wall just a short distance away from us on the left. Through the buzz and murmur of the creatures' unsettling style of communication, I suddenly heard a familiar voice.

It was Opeim.

I longed to run forward and free him at once, but that would have been suicide. These smaller creatures were not like the larger, warrior types, but still quite deadly in their own way. We needed a plan and, without our rifles, we needed something more than just knives to defend ourselves. I scooted out of sight, signaling for Tunuhun to follow me into the previous chamber. We needed to figure a way out of this and we needed to be quick about it. The longer we stayed in this underground warren, the more dangerous it became. My brain raced, trying to come up with a logical course of action as we returned to the cavern we'd fallen into the night before.

Once more illuminated by faint sunlight, I mused on how best to get out of the untenable situation we now found ourselves in. Deep in thought, my eyes followed the lines of the walls up to the rent in the ceiling. It would be a tough, if not impossible, climb to escape through that exit. I shook my head, thinking things through. We'd never make it out that way, especially if Opeim was injured and we were forced to carry him. Just what were these things anyway and why were they here?

Judging from the strata in the rock formations around us, this cave system, and the other structures we'd encountered thus far, had been sealed away for hundreds, perhaps even thousands of years. Like the mystery of the pyramids, I couldn't comprehend how these beings had created such smooth and perfectly geometric architecture. The strange tunnel that had appeared in the ravine with all those glowing, celestine pillars and now these chambers filled with interlocking panels depicting some sort of cultural record – all of it went well beyond my current level of understanding.

Were they from a time long ago, sealed away for countless eons, or did they come here from some other place entirely? Glancing at Tunuhun, I found him watching me with his usual calm confidence. It would seem that it was still my sole responsibility to see we made it safely through this ordeal.

I just didn't quite know where to begin.

Instead, I took stock of our situation. We had no firepower, very little in the way of supplies, and we were in an openly hostile environment. Our friend was in a room just down the hall, judging from the muffled sound of his voice, and we were surrounded on all sides by unfamiliar lifeforms. I took comfort in knowing that Opeim's voice, even though I hadn't been able to make out what he was saying, had been calm, conversational even. That must mean he was trying to communicate with these beings.

Could they be reasoned with? What about the ones we'd already killed? Would that be held against us if we tried to negotiate? And just how the hell were we supposed to start a dialogue with them to begin with?

As I stood wracking my brain, a sudden noise rose and fell like an alarm. It was shrill and then soft like steam from a train whistle, followed by the sound of a chainsaw at idle. I had no idea what the alternating sounds meant.

Turning, I signaled to Tunuhun. Then together we crept back toward the tunnel opening, hoping to discover just what the hell was going on.

-4-

As we reached the archway, I paused to peer around the edge once again. The color of the corridor had changed from a dull blue to a light orange and it seemed to be pulsating, almost beyond a spectrum visible to the naked eye. Most of the creatures were now scrambling down the hallway around the bend and out of our line of sight, while still others scuttled from the room on the left. Much to my relief, these were similar to the smaller ones we'd first encountered at the ravine; none of the larger variety were in evidence.

After a few more minutes, a heavy silence fell, the color of the corridor reverting to a blue hue that glowed with an etherealness that seemed a bit brighter than before. Motioning to Tunuhun, I drew my belt knife and crept forward, hugging the wall and heading in the direction the creatures had gone. Tunuhun positioned himself on the opposite side and inched toward the doorway. Upon reaching the portal, he glanced within and then gave the all-clear signal. Nodding, I continued, edging along the curve of the wall to see where the rest of the insectile beings had gotten to.

With the stealth of an experienced hunter, I slipped around the bend before settling into a crouch with my knife held at ready. Just down the corridor, I could see the last of the creatures congregating atop a platform that rested behind another archway. As I pondered on this strange development, the platform began vibrating with an electric hum. Then, in a sudden motion, it shot upward, carrying the creatures out of sight.

Moving forward down the now deserted hallway I glanced through the hexagonally-shaped archway to ensure there were no stragglers. Inside was a vertical, octagonally-shaped shaft about six feet across ringed by countless light blue striations. Leaning through the opening, I traced the lines of the empty shaft upward until they faded from sight. Perhaps this was some type of elevator? Shaking my head in disbelief, I hurried back the way I'd come.

Crouched by the other doorway, Tunuhun waited until I slipped up to the opening from the other side. With a nod, he then stood and eased into the room with his knife held steady before him. I followed a moment later, fervently hoping to find our companion. I didn't want to be here when those creatures returned.

The chamber we found ourselves in was like nothing I'd ever seen. Perfectly symmetrical geometric shapes formed much of the architecture and were harkened to in the construction of the room's other decorative elements. In the center of the chamber was an octagonal table with numerous small alcoves situated to either side along the walls. Each of these alcoves held a variety of unusual artifacts, but it was the table that drew my attention since pieces of Opeim's shredded clothing were laid out across it.

Glancing upward, I noted that hanging just above this platform was a series of small, semi-transparent panels which overlaid one another in an interlocking pattern. An additional unknown light source lit these panes from within and they glowed bright orange in the blue dimness of the room. From my vantage point, I could discern pictographs flowing across these thin plates, diagrams and enigmatic shapes swimming in and out of focus to my uncomprehending eyes as I stared on in growing wonder.

In that moment, I revised everything I thought I knew about these creatures. Thus far, I'd seen evidence of communication, architectural accomplishments, and a written pictographic language. Some of that could be explained away as ethological behavior since many species of known insects worked together to build structures and create things that could be viewed as decorative. But the colored lights, the elevator-like platform, and now this series of screens that appeared to be some type of advanced computer display all pointed to a much higher level of intelligence.

Were they an ancient, indigenous species that had been hidden away in the Brooks Range, only now to be dredged up by the earthquake, or were they something else entirely? I had to admit to myself that these things could be an alien species from some distant planet or perhaps even another reality altogether. It seemed far-fetched, stretching the limits of my own credulity, but what else could they be?

Cautiously venturing farther into the room, I studied the display panels situated just above the large table. Peering at the multitudinous screens from out of the corner of my eye, the images seemed to stretch and then merge together, blending the pictures on each pane into more detailed visual concepts. The images that they formed were not reassuring.

The interlocking diagrams depicted accurate and surprisingly precise maps of numerous biological systems of the human body. Laid out in successive schematics were the circulatory, nervous, renal, respiratory, skeletal, and reproductive systems. My estimation of these alien beings went up another notch. But there was only one way they could have gotten these meticulous representations of the intricate workings of our fleshy form.

Opeim.

Tracing the framework of the screens with my eyes, I followed the connections to the ceiling with some difficulty. The network was alien and, to my untrained eye, appeared vaguely organic in nature, embellished with knobs and protuberances that made me feel somewhat queasy. But by following them, I discovered that these pipes and tubules led into an adjacent room situated just to the left of us.

I signaled Tunuhun and together we moved to flank both sides of that hexagonal door frame. Then, with a brief jerk of my chin, I motioned for him to follow me inside. Peering around the edge of the door to make sure it was clear first, we slipped into the room.

Judging from the angle of the walls, this chamber also formed a geometric shape, perhaps another octagon. The diffuse lighting here was quite different though, more violet in color. Flattening myself against the wall beside the door, I decided to let my vision adjust to the strangeness of this new illumination before I continued.

As my eyes slowly became accustomed to the unusual lighting, I noticed thin sheets made of shimmering material coated in what looked to be labradorite hanging from the ceiling. They were flexible, like a shower curtain, yet more akin to a living membrane in appearance. Sparkling in the violet light, their iridescence almost blinded me as I moved cautiously into the chamber. These sheets, which were hung at odd angles to form a concentric ring, obscured whatever rested at the very center of this room. Pausing to glance back at Tunuhun, I motioned him forward and then proceeded with my exploration.

Moving through the sheets was disconcerting to say the least. The radiance shimmering off of them dazzled my eyes, while their rippling movements caused an uneasiness within me that I couldn't quite overcome. The light source grew brighter as we approached the middle, and I concentrated on making as little noise as possible as I wove in and out of the clinging, membranous partitions. Upon slipping through the last gelatinous curtain, I was filled with an all-consuming horror that I could feel all the way down to my very bones.

Before me were more illuminated screens, far larger than their counterparts in the previous room, set up in a vertical fashion from floor to ceiling. These panes were once again multitudinous, although I couldn't tell how many there were because they also interlocked like the ones in the outer chamber.

Their purpose, however, was eminently clear.

Like the images on the previous panels yet brought to life in vivid detail, my friend had been neatly sectioned, layer by layer. It was all extremely clean and sterile with no signs of blood or any other offal.

Moving around the display in morbid curiosity, I saw that most of the layers were of varying widths. I couldn't understand how it had been done. Each section displayed a separate system of his anatomy, some wider than others to accommodate the bulges of inner organs or bones, some thinner to show the intricate tracings of the circulatory and muscular systems. It was like someone had recreated pages from a medical textbook, but in real time. The contemplation of it left me stunned.

"Qaqisailaq."

The softly spoken observation startled me out of my reverie. Tunuhun had moved to stand beside the layer that housed most of Opeim's cranium. He was right again – the brains *were* missing.

I couldn't understand it. Only a few minutes ago, I had distinctly heard Opeim's voice. It'd been as though he was talking to his captors. How could they have done all this to him in so little time?

My mind flashed back to our time growing up together, scenes of us eating muktuk and giggling, our first hunt, the pride he'd felt when he'd downed his first caribou. So many, many images of the past floated behind my closed eyes. And now I would never see him again, never again have the pleasure of his company, or be able to rely on his precise marksmanship or steadfast friendship in times of need.

Anger swelled inside of me and grew until I could feel myself trembling with barely contained rage. These creatures – whatever the hell they were – they would pay for this! I promised myself, and his spirit, that I would do everything within my power to avenge him. The injustice of it all viscerally enraged me.

Leaning forward, I rested my free hand against the closest panel of the diabolical display, bowing my head while gripping the hilt of my hunting knife with the other so tightly that my knuckles cracked.

"Gillam, is that you?"

The unexpected echo of his voice shocked me out of my moment of silent brooding. It was disjointed and somewhat metallic, but it was also unquestionably Opeim. The sound of it set the hairs on the back of my neck to standing on end as Tunuhun dropped into a crouch, peering at the final, shimmering membrane that rested just beyond the ghastly series of anatomical displays. With a slow caution that was almost glacial in nature, he reached over and drew aside the last iridescent drapery.

Behind this final curtain rested a pillar of about five feet in height. It glowed with a faint, lavender radiance while a six-sided vessel about a foot and a half tall rested atop it. The upper and lower caps of this oddly configured container had more of the cryptic pictographs emblazoned along the edges, but the walls of it were made from a clear, crystalline substance similar to glass. Beads of moisture dotted its surface, forming tiny rivulets which ran down the semitransparent panes. As we stared at it, I began to make out a shape resting on the pedestal within.

It was a brain.

Just below this indistinctly displayed organ and dotted across the front of the glowing panel of condensation-covered crystal, was a honeycomb-shaped selection of holes. *"I knew you'd come for me,"* the voice said, floating outward in its faintly metallic tones from within those hollow divots. *"I've been waiting for you, Gillam..."*

-5-

I stared at the case that enclosed my friend's brain, wondering how it could still be animate. This room and everything we'd encountered so far mystified me. In all of the studies I'd ever undertaken, I'd never come across anything like the medical procedures we'd witnessed here in these chambers. Just what were these creatures and where did they come from? Was this mountain a fortified base of some sort?

Or was it simply a hive?

The more I thought about it, the less sense it made. In fact, I was now having trouble convincing myself that these things were even related to insects at all. The architecture that we'd seen, this technology, all of it went far beyond what lower forms of life, or even humans for that matter, were capable of. I was not a superstitious man and I'd always been skeptical about sentient beings outside of our own humanity, but for the life of me, I could think of no other way to categorize them. An intelligent, insect-like species living here on the planet, right under our noses, perhaps for hundreds of thousands of years – what were the odds? More importantly, what did they want and why were they here in the first place?

My mind grappled with these questions yet found no easy answers.

Stepping around the pylon, I ran my hands along the outside of the container, wiping the condensation off of the misted panels. On a short, metallic pedestal within the macabre apparatus rested Opeim's brain, wires and tubes connecting it to something located just beneath the container's bottom half. As I gazed at it, I noted that the organ still pulsed with visible life; it appeared that blood and other fluids were being supplied by the tubes coming from underneath the pedestal itself.

Whatever was going on in these foul catacombs, no matter what happened next, I knew one thing with utter certainty. They had done this horrible thing to my friend, a man whom I was responsible for, someone I was honor-bound to protect. Now I would make them pay for what they'd done, no matter the cost.

"Gillam?" the disembodied voice rang out again from the honeycomb-shaped speaker. *"Is that you? Is Tunuhun there with you?"*

Swallowing my surging emotions, I attempted to disconnect myself from my overpowering rage long enough to function coherently. "Yes," I replied through gritted teeth. "We're both here. What the hell have they done to you? How are you even still... alive?"

"They're taking me with them, back to the stars and beyond," came the metallic-sounding reply.

"They have shown me such sights, Gillam, things that you could not possibly imagine. And I will now go with them, traveling far from this world, journeying through the heavens to their home planet in a distant galaxy."

"What are you saying?" I cried out, unable to contain my frustrated confusion any longer. "I don't understand!"

"Be calm, "his voice whispered in its horrible, otherworldly sibilance. *"These creatures, they've never seen the likes of us before. Thousands of years ago, they came to our world, long before there were any humans living here. After they arrived, they built fortifications in many locations around the globe, for they were at war with another race, a star-traveling species like themselves. Their battles had raged on for many centuries, but this particular base was a scientific outpost, a research facility set at the opposite ends of the Earth from their foe's greatest strongholds. Here they perfected their advanced technology and made modifications to their own physiology in order to better fight in the ongoing war, in order to overcome their adversary's monstrous slave race of biologically-engineered soldiers. Then, during one of their sleep cycles, there was a great cataclysm. Their base was buried under tons of glacial ice and they fell into an uninterrupted self-induced slumber.*

"When they finally began awakening during that earthquake a few days ago, they discovered

they didn't recognize the world in which they now found themselves and neither could they make contact with any of their other bases that had once dotted the surface of this planet. After discovering our hunting party outside that ravine, they didn't know what to make of us. We have them confused, and they now argue amongst themselves. Gillam, there are thousands of them here, most still deeply asleep. But not for long, Gillam. Not for long. Any time now, they will decide what to do and then they will awaken their still sleeping soldiers, while simultaneously summoning further aide from the stars above. It's too late for me, but not for you, not for our tribe, and not for the planet either. The whole human race is at stake here, Gillam. You must stop them. You have to stop them!"

I didn't fully comprehend what he was saying, did not understand how any of it could be true. "How do you know all this?" I asked. "And why? Why have they done this terrible thing to you?"

"*Gillam,*" he replied. "*These things, they do not know us, do not yet understand who or what they're dealing with. They've tried to study me, have dissected my body, and now they've placed my mind into this device in order to transport my thoughts and ideas back to their home world. There, they will take me to speak with their leaders, their warlords. In order to convince them, they need proof; they need me to show that this planet is now controlled by a race that they've never before encountered. But Gillam, they do not know us! They didn't suspect that while they were communicating with me, sometimes mind-to-mind, learning our language and questioning me, that I'd be able to hear their thoughts as well, see into their own minds at the same time. I've witnessed many strange things, learned so much in such a short period of time that I can't even explain it all to you. I feel transcendent, as If I've been transformed into something else, something... new. It's like nothing that I've ever experienced before. But I know what they're doing now, know of their plans for our world I've somehow tapped into their hire intellect, and I tell you, Gillam, you have to stop them before this fortress can reach full power, before they can transmit a stronger signal back to their home planet."*

It was insane. This whole thing, it was just so completely unbelievable that my mind rebelled against it. Mystified, I watched as beads of moisture formed once again on the transparent panes of the container. As they ran down the smooth, geometric sides, I tried to rationalize what was happening. It was all too much, too fast. My thoughts skittered about in my head like penguins being chased by a pod of orcas.

Taking a deep, controlled breath, I calmed myself, gathering the scattered remnants of my fleeing intellect with desperate intent. This was a nightmare, but one from which I intended to escape. Glancing up, I caught Tunuhun's attention and then signaled him with my hand. He acknowledged my nonverbal instructions with a terse nod of his head, then crept off through the membranous curtains. I needed to know what else was in this room, find out if our enemies were returning. For that was what they were to me now – our sworn enemies. And I would destroy them all or die trying. I glanced down at my friend's brain now held secure within the luminescent vessel.

"What more can you tell us?" I asked. "Is there anything else we need to know in order to stop these creatures from what they're doing? Is there anything... anything at all... that we can do for you?"

"*I can tell you nothing more,* "Opeim replied. "*There is too much to process, too many confusing images twisting through my thoughts right now. All I really know for sure is that you must act quickly. Find a way up to the place where they're gathering. Distract them from their mission and then destroy them If you can. You cannot save me, but do not let my passing go unavenged.*"

Burning anger rose up in me once more, a bitterness that reached forth to strangle me with choking rage. Shaking with emotion, I gripped the sides of the container and pressed my forehead against its cool surface as I concentrated on nothing more than breathing deeply for the next few moments. Once I'd regained control of myself, I stepped back, running my hands down the misted, glowing sides of the octagonal device.

"We will never forget you, my friend," I said. "And you will not go unavenged. These creatures, we will stop them and find a way to interrupt that signal no matter what."

As I finished speaking, Tunuhun slipped back through the gelatinous sheets. Shaking his head, he gave the all-clear signal and then motioned that he'd continue his investigations in the previous set of rooms. With a gesture, I stopped him before he could leave.

"We need to stick together from now on, try and find weapons-" I began, but was interrupted by a change in the lighting. Everything pulsed rapidly within the chamber's violet glow and then we felt a thrum of rhythmic power, a deep vibration like the thunderous flow of a waterfall pouring down into an underground chasm.

Signaling Tunuhun to follow, I set out through the glimmering partitions, leaving what remained of my friend behind while a screaming void too painful to bear ripped opened within me. I knew I would have to come to grips with his death sooner or later, but now was not the time to dwell on such things. Hurrying through the room's arched entranceway, I passed the glowing display console and the platform which held Opium's gear and then went straight through the unexplored doorway at the back.

The place we found ourselves in was darker, illuminated only by the mysterious diffuse lighting that came from everywhere and nowhere at once. In the dimness I was still able to see that it was some kind of storage area. More of the geometric containers were stacked everywhere, many of them so large that they towered above us, while still others were no bigger than the palm of my hand. I had no idea what sort of biological specimens might be stored in them and found that at this point I was beyond caring.

Tunuhun stepped past me to snatch up a couple of long rods capped with triangular hoops from a rack leaning against a frosted glass case. Without hesitating, he began manhandling the triangles, bending them from side to side, working the unfamiliar metal back and forth until they snapped from their shafts. Turning toward me, he offered me one and I took it, studying it in the dim lighting.

It was a type of alloy I couldn't identify, but the broken, jagged point at the top now made for a wicked-looking spear. Grunting in satisfaction, I motioned for him to precede me, and then together we left the room without another look back. I had no desire to gaze through any of the mist-covered, transparent panes of this massive collection of different sized, hermetically-sealed canisters. I found that I didn't really want to know what else these creatures had been collecting when they'd last been free to roam the stars unchallenged.

Moving toward the main exit, we passed the table and monitors, then paused at the threshold of the outer doorway. The air still vibrated with that roaring thrum, the lights pulsing in violent discord. I didn't know what it meant, but there was no sense in taking any chances. Leaning against the wall to either side of the door, we carefully peered into the corridor.

And found it to be deserted.

Breathing a sigh of relief, I motioned to Tunuhun and we crept down the hallway toward the room that I'd seen the other creatures departing from earlier. If it was some type of elevator, I intended to find out how it worked and use it to travel to whatever place above us they now congregated in. There had to be some way, I was sure, that we could use our vast array of hunting skills to an advantage once we'd found out where these creatures were holding their councils. It could mean the difference between life and death, but we had trusted in our abilities on many different hunts before this and always prevailed. I decided right then and there that we would track these things down like animals, taking them out one-by-one if we had to. It was these thoughts of imminent revenge which now drove me forward with little further regard for my own personal safety.

As we traveled down the corridor, I could see that there were no other markings, doorways, or indentations that would indicate potential exits from this section of the creatures' base. I knew that taking the platform would be risky. If they were gathered just at the top of the shaft, we could be in big trouble. I pondered on all of this before reaching its hexagonal entrance. Was there some other way to get to the top of this mountain? If we did manage to figure out how to use the elevator, how could we control our assent? These questions and more flitted through my mind as Tunuhun slipped into the compartment beside me and knelt to study the floor. Turning his head, he shot me a look of inquiry.

Using hand signals, I let him know that this platform would take us upward. He nodded at that and then returned to his silent perusal of the room around us.

Could there be another way, a safer way, to get to the top of this place? I wondered as I studied the chamber myself. It was octagonal in shape, but the walls were as smooth as polished glass, the striations running through them vivid and glowing with inner light. Their appearance reminded me of core samples I'd seen taken from solid bedrock during a geological expedition I'd once been on. I did a slow turn about the space, searching for any other markings or engravings, buttons or controls, that would give us access to the lift's power, yet I found nothing inscribed upon the pristine, cold surfaces that surrounded us.

The tube lining the shaft seemed to be made from more of the transparent substance that we'd seen used in the brain canisters. I didn't know if it was glass or some type of synthetic polymer. Peering upward into the dimness, I focused on the lights winking far above us. They glowed like distant stars, revealing no ladder or other handholds along the sides of the shaft that I could see. I was left at a loss as to how we were supposed to proceed.

Shaking my head in consternation, I glanced back down and noticed Tunuhun running his belt knife along the crack between the floor and the wall. There wasn't even enough room for his sharp-tipped blade to slip between the fitted stone and the side of the tube. He grunted once and then sat back on his haunches, raising an eyebrow at me. It was my call.

I did another slow turn about the space, searching for something, anything that would give me a clue as to how we'd get this elevator moving. Glancing upward again, I saw the enclosed shaft ran straight to the top and then opened into an area high above us. From this distance though, it was just a pinpoint of illumination, a tiny patch of glowing light at the end of a long, vaguely luminescent tunnel. I was beginning to get a bad feeling about all of this. Maybe it wasn't such a good idea to go right to the apex of this place and confront beings that had access to far more advanced technology than we ourselves possessed. Now that we had only our wits and a few simple tools to rely upon, it seemed like utter madness.

We had to either find another way to make it to the areas above or go back and see if we could discover more information, or at least better weapons, in the cave with the large pictographic panels. I was just deciding that this might be our best course of action when a chime loud enough to be heard over the rhythmic thrum sounded from all around us. With an electronic whir, the platform shot upward, causing the both of us to stumble from the sudden inertia.

Whether we liked it or not, we were on our way to the top.

I didn't know just how fast we were moving, but the lift rose through the tube at a smooth, even pace. Soon, we shot past the lip of the lower end of the shaft that was drilled down into the surrounding bedrock and then we were rising through an immense cavity which opened up beyond the elevator's transparent siding. The view thus revealed shook me to the very core of my being.

The entire interior of this artificial mountain was built like a hive. Within thousands upon thousands of octagonal frames were innumerable cell clusters, housed like the inside of a bee's honeycomb. These interlocking panels were immense, bigger than I could have ever imagined, stretching off in all directions into the infinite shadows. At first, there appeared to be no order to them, but as I stepped back to get a wider view, the pattern became more apparent. All the cells were carefully orchestrated to form one gigantic geometric design, almost like the Mandelbrot set. There were other tubes like the one we were in spaced at regular intervals around the walls, and lights from above and below lit the open space with a soft, purplish radiance.

Curious as to how far-reaching the space was, I moved to the edge of the platform and peered down. In the very center at the bottom of this mountainous stronghold stood an enormous profusion of the glowing crystalline pillars that we'd seen outside of the exit tunnel in the ravine. Was it some type of energy source? Its centrality seemed to suggest so, but there was no way for me to know for sure.

From far above us, there came a blue pulsation of light emanating from what appeared to be a sizeable orb. As we rose through this massive chamber of incomprehensible technology, a terror built inside me with a magnitude that I had not yet experienced. All this time the things we'd witnessed had stunned me so deeply that I'd been living in a constant state of denial; it was only now that the fear had finally caught up to me. The chilling realization of what we were doing, the insidious knowledge of the things we were up against – how were we going to prevail against such odds?

In a mild stupor, I edged away from the side of the tube and moved to stand by the hexagonal exit arch. As the cell clusters to either side of us slid past,

I tried to distance myself from the immensity of the surrounding hive by focusing only on their current occupants. They all seemed to be filled with the warrior versions of these strange, insectile creatures and I realized that if we didn't stop them, these things could very well become active, could awaken and then leave this nest in droves. The thought of it sent a further chill racing through my veins.

As I stood there, dumbstruck by the horror of it all, some of the darkened cells began to flicker and then illuminate from within.

With overwhelming dismay, I realized the sleeping insectile beings were reanimating at an exponential rate, the lights flashing in a rapidly repeated pattern all across the interior of this infernal fortress of long-lost alien antagonists. With a trembling surety that I could no longer control, I knew, deep in my bones, that we were already too late to stop them.

-6-

As the lift slid to a smooth and effortless stop, I hefted the spear and positioned myself next to the archway. Tunuhun was already balanced on the balls of his feet, holding his own weapon overhead so that it angled down toward the opening. If anything chose to come at us from any direction, it would be in for a rude awakening. I'd seen that pose a hundred times before and he was as accurate a man as I'd ever known with a harpoon. Glancing a final time at the massive cluster of awakening hibernation cells glowing to life beyond the tube's transparent siding, I pressed my back against the wall and then glanced around the edge of the exit.

Before me was a short corridor ending at a cross section. From where I stood, I could see a group of the smaller creatures standing next to some complex machinery situated in a large chamber just to the other side of the hallway intersection. With the lights still flashing and the vibrant rush of the roaring, waterfall-like reverberations, the scene took on an even more otherworldly quality as I stood considering our next course of action.

Then suddenly, the rushing noise stopped altogether. The orange lights transitioned back to a steady blue and the creatures paused what they were doing before scuttling down the hallway to their left. Only one or two remained at the controls of whatever great machine it was they were manipulating, but I figured now was our best chance to slip past them. Giving Tunuhun the signal to proceed, we turned the corners of the lift's hexagonal entrance and crept to the end of the short hallway.

Crouching at either side of the connecting tunnel, we peered around the corners. To the left, the longer hallway stretched off into the distance, but there was also another doorway a little ways down from us on the opposite side. Glancing to the right, I noted that the other end of the corridor gave way onto a large, open area. This appeared to be some sort of immense platform suspended above the interior cavity through which we'd just risen and it was packed with the smaller creatures milling about in an agitated state. Before them all, floating in the air, was an enormous globe filled with radiant, lavender-colored energy.

As I watched on in mounting horror, an image formed within that glowing sphere, massive and unfathomable to me in its ever-shifting loathsomeness. I had to tear my eyes away from it lest I go mad just from viewing the abysmal thing. But before I could lose myself completely to my slipping sanity I felt a hand clench my shoulder. It was Tunuhun, his eyes shadowed now with a fear I'd never thought to see in the man.

Giving me a brusque upward jerk of his chin, he indicated that we should follow the hallway to the left. I needed no more prompting to do so and hurried from the hideous sight of the being that was now taking shape in the center of that accursed globe as quickly as I could. As we slipped past the two remaining creatures still operating the machinery in the chamber across the hall, from behind us there came the sounds of a laborious voice booming out in echoing waves of incomprehensible gibberish.

With that hellish discourse driving us onward, we hastened down the corridor to the left. We had to find a safe place to regroup, somewhere we could plan out our next move without the constant threat of discovery. As we came abreast of the unexplored room, we fanned out, taking up positions on either side of the archway before peering around its edges.

It was another chamber filled with convoluted equipment and more of those octagonally-shaped screens, with large containers like the ones we'd seen in the storage room taking up most of the remaining space. There were hundreds of them sitting in ordered rows here with shadowy, shapeless figures held immobile behind their glistening, frost-covered windows. Scanning the rest of the area, I noticed their display screens crawled with unfamiliar data and many of the containers also had bio-luminescent wiring running out into side consoles situated just below the clustered panels themselves.

We crept into the room, spears held at ready, but the chamber appeared empty of any *living* beings. All of the insectoid creatures must have been called away to communicate with whatever was forming inside that massive globe suspended above the central hive. Just the thought of its writhing visage made me cringe, my thoughts skittering away from the memory as I tried desperately not to think on it. Fighting down my almost inescapable dread, I approached the nearest of the multilayered monitors to study the jumble of otherworldly symbols and pictographs glowing bright orange as they scrolled across the sequentially-spaced screens.

These were similar to the smaller displays we'd seen below in the dissection room, yet different, more complex, and adorned with many additional interlocking layers. The information being correlated there was extensive but the cross-sections showed creatures that I vaguely recognized for some strange reason. Barrel-shaped and marked with vertically furrowed striations, the beasts had irregular, star-shaped heads with eyes and eating tubes located at the tips of each arm. In addition to that, they also had what appeared to be a series of fleshy pseudopods radiating out from the base of their torpid bodies, possibly used for locomotion. I could make no sense of what I was seeing. Was this a variety of overgrown sea creature, or was it yet another sentient lifeform that had also existed here thousands of years ago? I had no way of telling, although a vague recollection of having seen these beings before tickled at the back of my mind.

The more I studied the diagrams and glowing pictographs stacked one upon the other, the more unsettled I became. Turning away from these maddening images, I sought to share my findings with Tunuhun, but was just in time to see him disappearing through a small, hexagonal archway that I'd not noticed earlier. As he ventured farther into the next room, a series of lights flickered to life, illuminating a large window located on the wall next to me. What I saw within the chamber beyond made me tremble in shocked disbelief.

The interior of the adjacent area was set up similar to the one in which we'd first found Opie, yet it was different in many chilling ways. I was struck by a surety that I hadn't felt since we'd gotten here that this was a place of torture, a room the beings who'd built this foul base had used for the sole purpose of interrogation. Strapped to a low table in the middle of the chamber was one of the starfish-headed creatures currently being displayed on the screens all around me. With a suddenness that caused me to stumble and clutch at a nearby instrument tray for support, I realized then what I was seeing.

These were the ancient enemies of the insect-like beings, the ones that had been depicted on the historical record slabs within the cavern we'd fallen into the night before.

My mind shied away from the knowledge that we were encountering not one, but two forms of life that were as yet unknown to the race of men. Staggering over to the window, I placed one hand on the wall to steady myself while setting my spear on a nearby ledge. As I watched with detached interest, Tunuhun approached the platform and reached toward the unusual bindings which held the thing restrained. In that moment, an irrepressible feeling of imminent danger flashed through my mind, compelling me to immediate action.

Breaking into a run, I dashed into the chamber, reaching him before he could get close enough to touch the heavy straps and then grabbing his arm to stop him. His eyes were glossy in the strange blue lighting, his muscles tightening under my hand as if he were about to rip free of my grasp. Shaking his head, he turned on me with a fearsome look, a snarl almost curling his lips as he spoke.

"Allagi."

"I know this one is different from the others," I agreed, "but that does not make it any less dangerous for us to handle. We don't even know what this thing is!"

"Anipkaq!"

I was unprepared for him to insist on releasing it. Just what was going on behind those cold, dark eyes, I had no idea, but as I considered his demand, I began to realize that these beings were the true prisoners here. Trapped for so many thousands of years, tortured and brutalized by their enemies before that, even in death they were denied any sort of dignity. I glanced down at the ancient, well-preserved corpse lying on the platform next to me, studying its physiology, noting the strips of rubbery skin missing from its body and the strange devices inserted into its desiccated flesh. It wasn't quite pity that I felt, yet there was an undeniable sense of wrongness about this whole series of rooms, a feeling of absolute despair hanging like a pall over this entire area. Perhaps it would do no harm to unbind the shackles holding the creature secure to this diabolical table. In its present condition, it could feel nothing about it one way or the other, but perhaps its spirit would be able to find what little semblance of peace these things had in whatever afterlife they shared. I decided it could do no harm.

It was as I reached out toward the closest strap that one of the creature's abdominal tentacles unrolled from its rigid state, an unexpected curl of movement not unlike the frond of a fern unfurling in the light of the morning sun. My eyes tracked it without fully comprehending the danger until it was too late. Lashing out, this slimy, puckered, and pebbled appendage wrapped itself firmly around my wrist. As the thing's textured skin clasped my own flesh, its suckers clamping onto me with a finality that took my breath away, a series of images flooded my mind, sending me spiraling into a maelstrom of alien thoughts and ideas.

I was lost, submerged within a vast reservoir of memories that were so foreign to me that I could not distinguish where they ended and I now began. The experiences of this strange being drowned me in an ongoing deluge of perceptions that the human intellect was never meant to comprehend. I was somewhat aware of Tunuhun calling my name, but it came to me as if from over a great distance, like I'd been transported into another realm overlaying that of our own humble existence here on Earth, yet encapsulating it within a larger, more diverse reality. Flailing through this overwhelming amount of sensory data, my mind seemed to shatter into a million tiny pieces, spiraling outward through a never-ending stream of time and space to intermingle with the incalculable expanse of this captive creature's consciousness.

It was like being tossed into a raging river of unlimited knowledge, an informational flood that swept me away in its unbreakable grasp. I was within the creature's mind as it was within my own, a simultaneous exchange, and one that I could sense was almost as confusing to it as it was to myself. Its thought patterns went far beyond the limited understanding of my fragile, human mind, such a large and strangely ordered mentality that I despaired of ever retaining my own true identity.

The things I saw – places, star charts, and images of its past – all melded together, carrying me further and further from my own sense of self, tumbling my unraveling individuality through a fierce deluge of life experiences that had happened to a far greater intelligence than my own.

Just as I thought I'd never again find myself amidst this cascading cataract of concepts, the creature riffled through my thoughts a final time, gathered up the pieces of my fractured self, and then thrust them all back into my own body once more. As it released its hold upon my wrist, it made a sound like the plaintive call of a box of half-drown kittens, a thin, mewling intonation that set my teeth on edge as I stumbled away from it. Unable to withstand even his familiar touch upon my overstimulated flesh, I shook off Tunuhun's offer of support, fetching up against the opposite wall instead. There I found a large, round window like a ship's porthole and, closing my eyes tight against the throbbing pain in my head, I placed my forehead against this welcome sheet of moisture-streaked glass, cooling my overheated skin upon its icy surface.

Images still slid past behind my closed eyes, stunning me with the intricacies of this being's life and the depth of its foreign dreams. I saw worlds beyond imagining, sights and sounds and colors I could not hope to fully process within a single lifetime. In that instant I found myself sliding closer to madness than I'd ever been before. Quaking in mind, body, and spirit, I clutched at the cold surface of the window, shaking as I tried to regain some sense of my true identity once more.

Yet, even through the confusion and pain, pieces of the data I'd adsorbed began to fall into place. For instance, I knew now that these creatures were from the stars, a space-faring race that had migrated here hundreds of thousands of years ago while fleeing persecution from a power even greater than themselves. They'd fought many battles and had built great cities here upon Earth with the help of the minions they'd created. I had only the remotest sense of what this other servitor race was like, vivid flashes of semi-elastic bodies able to expand and form appendages at will, huge amorphous beings that were the very stuff of eldritch nightmare.

Shuddering uncontrollably, I ripped my thoughts away from this unintended trip back through the mind of the captive creature, seeking to reestablish a sense of equilibrium, to fight against drowning again in the memories of a being that was so far beyond my understanding. It struck me then that there was hot liquid oozing down my chilled features and I latched onto that distraction, reaching up to dab at my face with trembling hands. Opening my eyes, I found blood on my fingertips. With a gasp, I sought out my reflection in the glass before me and I saw there that I now bled from my eyes, ears, nose, and mouth.

Wiping frantically at the blood streaming down my face, I tried to calm my racing heart, but as I gazed at my image in the round pane of glass, something just beyond that transparent panel caught at my attention, something that swirled and eddied within whatever otherworldly environment lay hidden behind such a curiously placed porthole. Leaning forward, I peered deeper into the viscus-looking, grayish-green murkiness and began to see patterns in the depths, tendrils and ligaments forming and reforming while ropes of fleshy material slid across the other side of the glass itself. Suddenly, an eye appeared from out of that bottomless abyss like the ocular orb of some gargantuan cephalopod, staring back at me with an intensity that went far beyond simple animalistic curiosity. No, this was a look of pure sentience, I was sure, and as I gaped at this sudden apparition, stumbling backward into Tunuhun's waiting arms, I saw the eye change, reforming itself into an exact duplicate of my own.

With a moan, I collapsed into oblivion, my mind unable to handle anything more.

-7-

My eyes were sticky with dried blood and my head
spinning as I swam back up into consciousness.
It took me a moment to get my bearings, to clear
my mind enough to think. Without moving, I took
stock of my surroundings. I was now laying on the
floor, a folded parka placed beneath my aching head.
The images and excessive amounts of otherworldly
knowledge I'd absorbed from the ancient lifeform
had receded, but I could still feel it as a pressure just
behind my closed eyes. I had no idea how this new
layer of perception would continue to affect me, but
for now, I was grateful it hadn't destroyed my mind
or changed me in any more noticeable ways. At least
as far as I could tell. I was going to be alright – for
now. Glancing around, I tried to determine what was
going on, how long I'd been unconscious.

It must not have been for very long. I found that
I now lay behind the collection of storage tanks we'd
seen in the first chamber and realized Tunuhun must
have carried me here after I'd passed out. With a
great amount of cautious optimism, I sat up, raising
my hands to my head to probe my skull with gentle
fingers. There seemed to be no additional bumps

or other contusions besides the ones I'd sustained during the fall last night, so perhaps I was as fit as I was going to be for the time being. The spare medical kit rested beside me and a wad of soiled antiseptic wipes told me that Tunuhun had cleaned the blood from my face and hands while I was out. The parka I'd been lying on was his and I found him sitting cross-legged just behind me, his broad back propped against the wall as he worked.

We were hidden from view of the hallway in this corner of the room, and I met his eyes with a look of gratitude I knew he'd be able to fathom just from my expression alone. He nodded to me before returning to what he'd been doing, and as I studied the objects he now held, my knowledge of basic chemistry came back to me in a rush.

Stripped to the waist, muscles gleaming in the light of the blackout torches, he was emptying the spare ammo cartridges onto a slip of folded paper. Other items from our limited supplies were placed on the floor around him and from their composition, I could tell he was fashioning an incendiary device of some sort. His spear was set across his knees at an angle and he'd already built a serviceable delivery system around the shaft near the tip. It was apparent he was making a weapon that could explode upon impact, using the emergency flares, gun powder, fuses, flashlight batteries, and other chemicals from our medical supplies. His features were shadowed and grim, the tracings of many scars from old injuries that he'd sustained during past hunts standing out across his rock-hard body. The lines of his face and set of his jaw showed me that he was determined, and he'd tied back his long, sable hair to keep it from falling into his eyes as he worked.

Watching him there, his nimble fingers piecing together the foundations of the destructive force he hoped to unleash, I was reminded of something intrinsically primal – a lone warrior preparing for battle against overwhelming odds.

Shifting my position, I peeked around the tanks we were hidden behind. The room was quiet with only the distant sounds of the globe creature's guttural discourse filling the silence around us. Glancing toward the chamber located across from me, I winced as I spied the barrel-shaped, star-headed prisoner still lying strapped to the table. It came to me then that the containers stacked in orderly rows beside me held others of its kind, all trapped here, all captured on a raiding mission eons ago. While within the massive cell built behind the wall on the other side of that room of torture and pain rested one of their servants, a member of their biologically engineered slave race bound here with them for all eternity.

I shuddered away from the thought of my own eye gazing back at me from within that vile holding tank. How I knew all these things, I couldn't say for sure, but the images were quite clear to me for a moment before I pulled my mind away from the memories, blocking them from further consideration while hoping to limit any additional damage to my fragile psyche. They say that the enemy of your enemy is your friend, but I was truly out of my depth in this situation, and I wanted nothing more to do with this captive creature's confusing mental manipulations.

I simply wanted revenge.

Opeim had been right; we needed to put a stop to whatever was going on at the end of the main corridor as soon as possible. It was hard for me to say if the globe was even a part of it, but their attempts at communicating with their home planet had to be interrupted and the base itself destroyed if we could manage it. I just didn't know how we were going to go about such a monumental task. With a sinking heart, I realized that we needed to scout out the situation to achieve a better understanding of what we were up against. It was obvious the odds were stacked against us, but with our combined hunting and survival skills, I was confident we could find some way to slow these creatures down long enough for the military to take over – even if it cost us our lives in doing so. My own sanity was already questionable at this point seeing as how I could no longer tell where my own thoughts ended and the captive creature's influence began. The only thing I did know with any certainty was that we had to somehow succeed.

Climbing to my feet, I scouted around the room, hoping to find something – anything – we could use. There was nothing that would be of immediate service to us, so I rejoined my friend as he wrapped the end of his spear, securing the rest of the device he'd cobbled together with a small roll of medical tape. It looked makeshift to my eyes, but I trusted Tunuhun to know what he was doing.

Leaning down, I picked up his parka and held it out to him. He propped the spear against the wall before shrugging back into his thermal undershirt. Then he took the jacket from my hands, tying it around his waist while staring back at me with a questioning look. It was hot in these chambers, but I was chilled to the bone regardless.

Deciding to leave my parka on, I chose its added warmth and padded protection over the comfort and freedom of movement that removing it would have offered me. Then, gathering up my own spear from the corner where Tunuhun had placed it, I motioned to him and we set out for the main hallway.

Peering around the corner of the archway, I found the last remaining creatures were scuttling from the room just down the corridor. They appeared to be heading for the large platform at the other end of the long hallway to join others of their kind that were gathering there. The purple-blue globe floating above that vast area was glowing, its pulsating light and ominous, guttural cacophony adding an additional layer of apprehension to the way I already felt. With fear knotting my insides, I set out for the room they'd so recently vacated. Perhaps we'd find something there to assist us in thwarting their plans; maybe we would even be able to interrupt the transmission they were attempting to send. It was a weak plan, but the only one I had for now, so I went with it.

We sidled down the passageway, taking care to remain unseen, but I shouldn't have worried. The creatures were so intent upon that hellish face forming within the gigantic sphere that none of them even turned our way as we slid around the corner of the archway and into the room beyond.

The new chamber was immense and, similar to the previous rooms, filled with interconnected flat panels and mechanical devices. The only difference here was the size and abundance with which the screens and monitors adorned the cavernous area.

Several of the largest ones dominated the center of the chamber, while still others were distributed about in what, at first, struck me as a random pattern. In addition to these illuminated panels showing a variety of data that flickered and scrolled across each separate leaf, there were also other geometrically-shaped platforms and work benches accompanied by more of those celestite pillars which thrust up through the floor in glowing clusters. Glancing upward, I saw that the walls disappeared into shadowy gantries far above, hidden by darkness and containing many pipes and ducts that ran from machines situated around the walls. At the edges of the raised, central dais stood rows of tall, octagonally-sided containers filled with syrupy liquid swirling with motes of light that reminded me of hundreds of fireflies trapped within jars. The fluid itself was blue in color, but continually changed hues as I watched. The concoction burbled and flashed as the groupings of lights within it surged apart and then clustered back together, breaking away from each other and reforming again in a never-ending cycle.

Amongst the other odd-shaped structures that lined the walls were also immense bladders of indeterminate origin that billowed in and out like living, breathing organisms. I didn't quite know what to make of it all. Stepping onto the main dais, I saw from its raised height that all of the objects placed within this chamber were positioned in such a way that they formed a much larger pattern, one that was also geometric in design and must have had some function that was not immediately clear to me. Signaling Tunuhun to scout around, I stepped over to the main control panel.

The markings here were quite bold, yet gave no indication of how the machine was supposed to be operated. Studying its configuration, I noted that the platform was octagonal in shape with a raised surface that tilted at a 45-degree angle and a base which melded seamlessly into the floor. The spongy-looking, triangular indentations that covered it were arranged in a decorative fashion with many of them spaced apart at equal intervals. In addition to the holes and divots, the top of it was etched with red and yellow diagrams, markings that had a significance I was sure, yet told me nothing of how the machine was supposed to function. As I considered the problem, I realized that the triangular depressions were about the right size for claw tips. These creatures had an abundance of different appendages that were shaped in such a way and so it struck me that they'd have no difficulty at all in accessing these recessed areas. I stuck my finger into one of the apertures, but was unable to reach whatever toggle rested at the very bottom. Jabbing my spear tip into the hole had similar disappointing results. I could see no other way to gain access and spent a frustrating few minutes trying everything I could think of just to reach these recessed buttons and switches. After repeated failures, I gave up and instead studied the huge, glowing screens that were suspended from the ceiling in front of me.

The data flowing past was too detailed and complex for me to puzzle out. Charts, diagrams, long strings of shapes and other angular designs I could only assume were writing scrolled by, collecting and correlating across multiple layers in convoluted patterns. I glanced around, searching for something familiar, something I could understand, something I could make use of to destroy this central unit. The other, smaller screens processed data in much the same way but gave me no clue as to how I was to proceed. Baffled, I once more searched the room and my eyes were drawn back to the colored tubes with their sparkling interior lights.

Moving to the nearest burbling collection of tanks, I searched around the bases of them, seeking to discover how they were attached to the apparatus upon which they rested. There I found a series of membranous, flesh-colored flaps spreading outward from the bottom of each vessel forming what appeared to be gaskets. As I looked on in mounting disgust, I saw fluids flowing through these membranes in multicolored tubules almost like blood vessels. Setting down my spear, I wrapped my arms around the central container and began twisting and pulling at it. There was some give, but the tall, fluid-filled object refused to budge more than a few inches at best.

Taking up my spear again, I ran the tip of it around the bottom edge of the flap, separating the membrane from the shaft, and was promptly rewarded with a spurt of foul-smelling liquids that shot up to drench my face and hands. It was disgusting, but I didn't let it stop me as I continued to cut and pry at the skin-like tissues. After a few moments, the gasket released its hold on the transparent siding and I was able to twist it, tipping it from side to side. The weight of it was too much for me though, so I moved around behind it and put my back against another machine while placing my feet up on the side of the tank itself. Then, pushing with all of my might, I strained to tilt the object over onto the main control panel.

Inch by inch the wretched thing began to give way and, after a few moments of intense effort, the whole container toppled forward, falling onto the main platform and cracking in several places. As colored liquids began gurgling from these hairline fractures, the top of the cylinder broke off, sending gallons more chugging out in a sluggish tidal wave across the controls.

Circling the remaining tanks, I looked to see what my attempt at sabotage had wrought. The colored lights from within the tube had become more identifiable as I studied them in astonished distaste. They appeared to be semi-aquatic, insectile organisms not native to our world. Crawling about in the viscous residue, the organisms' inner lights fluctuated as they sought to re-group themselves into viable patterns once more. When they failed to achieve this symmetry of purpose in their new environment, they raced around the panel with a dizzying swiftness until they found cracks and crevices to scuttle into. Many of them disappeared inside the indentations I'd tried earlier to access. I hoped this combination of spillage and small, detestable creatures would be of some help in deactivating whatever great mechanism this central unit was.

Pausing a moment while I caught my breath, I watched the glowing panels and observed the control surface which was now awash in bluish goop for any changes, yet there were none that I could recognize with the naked eye. The information on the huge, multilayered screens continued to flash by, the images and diagrams accompanied with incomprehensible writing scrolling across the flat surfaces with no noticeable deviation. The disappointment I felt was considerable.

There had to be some way to interrupt the signal they were sending, but I wasn't sure if this machine had anything to do with their transmission at all. I was just going off of gut instinct at this point. But those insect-like creatures had been clustered together in this very room when we'd first stepped off of the elevator. The noises we'd been hearing, and even now continued to hear, had all started right after we'd seen them manipulating these controls. Following that, we'd witnessed many of them leaving to go to the end of the hallway where the giant globe was located. The room itself was in close proximity to the globe, so after adding it all up, I was reasonably certain this device had something to do with the transmission of their communication signal. We just had to figure out a way to deactivate or interrupt it. As I stood pondering all of this, something caught at my attention from the corner of my eye.

Turning, I noticed subtle changes were occurring within the remaining unbroken, fluid-filled vessels. The tube I'd toppled had been in the center of one of the strange configurations of interconnected containers. Those left to either side of the gap were beginning to swirl and flash at a reduced speed. As I watched on, the organisms inside the remaining tanks began to split up, the patterns they once formed breaking apart to become disjointed. I also realized that the color was off. Once a variety of ever-changing, vibrant blue hues, the swirling liquids had taken on a slightly more brownish color. There was something happening alright, I just didn't know what it was.

Glancing back at the overlapping screens, I witnessed changes happening there as well. The ones at the back of the group had gone dark, followed by some of those that were situated in the very middle. The information scrolling across all of them seemed dependent upon each separate leaf to complete the images being shown, and once those layers blinked out, a cascade of further degradation inflicted the remaining data. In an awed state of shock, I watched as the chaos I'd created multiplied across the entire series of panels – and then became deeply afraid. What would result from this interruption of their main computing functions? I didn't plan on being around long enough to find out. My head swiveled back and forth seeking any avenue of escape as I backed away from the ongoing destruction I'd initiated.

Stumbling off the edge of the raised dais, I caught my balance just as the lights within the room began to flicker in a strobe-like pattern. Tunuhun came racing around the side of one of the peculiar machines resting along the back wall, his eyes wide in shocked confusion. My whole attempt at damaging their central processing unit had taken only a few moments while he'd been scouting the room, but now he motioned for me to follow him without further delay. Wasting no more time, I hefted my spear and ran, for in the corridor outside of this otherworldly chamber I could already hear the dickering scuttle of multiple sets of claws as the creatures scrambled down the hallway, seeking to discover, no doubt, what had happened to their malfunctioning equipment.

The machine Tunuhun stood beside was almost as tall as he was. Upon reaching him, we both ducked behind it and then proceeded along a short pathway which ended at a hexagonal aperture in the back wall. Was this some sort of service tunnel? I had no idea. I only knew that the noises were becoming louder by the minute; I could already hear the weird strains of other sounds intermixed, the buzzing and clicking of outraged beings now filling the room behind us. It was with a vast sense of relief that I left with Tunuhun through the small archway, both of us running deeper into the darkened passageway which burrowed straight into the solid rock of the artificial mountain's crust.

Behind us, the chittering increased in volume, picking up a great deal of angry hissing in addition to the buzzing and clicking. Other sounds accompanied these noises as well, like a large number of agitated beings shuffling about, perhaps even now working to repair the damage I'd wrought. Undoubtedly, they'd soon be searching for us in earnest. With these thoughts of imminent pursuit utmost in my mind, we continued down the cramped corridor and flew up a series of interlocking ramps to come out onto a group of gantries overlooking the hive's central chamber with the sphere platform just below us. The view from this suspended walkway filled me with equal amounts of fear and awestruck wonder as I gazed out at the colossal dimensions of this epically proportioned subterranean acropolis.

It was clear to me now that I'd underestimated the immensity of the mountain's internal cavity when we'd ascended in the elevator's tube. Seeing it now from this vantage point however, I was forced to reconsider the vast extent of it all and what that meant for the continued survival of the human race. The outer shell of the base itself was gigantic, having thrust itself up within the Brooks Range to an even greater height than the peaks around it. From within the lift we'd only had a partial glimpse of the interior, but now a panoramic view opened up beneath me.

As far as my eye could see in every direction was a cavern which dwarfed anything I'd ever previously encountered. It was entirely hollow, only the sides of it being honeycombed by interconnected rooms, and now this great void stretched out before me like the emptiness of interstellar space. It was only because of the crystalline pillars at the very bottom, the prolific amount of hive cells now winking into life on every wall, and the glowing lines of illuminated, equally-spaced transport tubes around the circumference that I was even able to finally grasp its overall size. To say that I was shocked would have been a tremendous understatement.

Forcing myself to look away from the thousands upon thousands of hibernation cell clusters which clung to every crack and crevice in patterns that both confused yet delighted my senses, I focused my attention upon the platform below. Right now, I could waste no more time in worrying about the creatures who were already awakening. I needed to concentrate on making sure reinforcements from their home planet would never arrive. And so, it was to that effort that I bent my every thought now as I studied the problem from the gantries above.

Swarming around the globe below us were a great many of the insectoids, both the larger, more heavily armored types as well as the smaller, flightless variety. The sphere itself was immense, filled with glowing, violet-colored gasses and more of those sparkling, lightning bug-like creatures I'd seen in the room from which we'd just escaped. Inside of this apparatus of unknown function floated the face of a lifeform that my fragile, human intellect could not comprehend, let alone continue to contemplate without suffering long-lasting mental trauma. Suffice it to say that this being was repulsive beyond imagining, a writhing collection of tentacles, multifaceted eyes, and serrated mandibles that stretched my psychological fortitude right to the breaking point.

Averting my gaze, I instead concentrated on the sphere itself and on the connections hanging down from someplace far above which attached the entire globe to whatever power source it needed to remain active. Of course, this was all supposition on my part, but I had an almost premonition-like certainty that it was somehow linked to their communications system, so I pointed out this joining of unfamiliar technologies to Tunuhun who stood beside me studying the situation.

His expression, always impassive even at the worst of times, had now taken on a look of silent loathing, which made his features seem even more severe in the violet glow of the immense sphere. Following the point of my outstretched fingertip, he grasped the situation at once, moving into a stance I knew only too well from our days of whaling. Muscles bulging beneath his sweat-stained thermal shirt, he sighted down at the junction of the apparatus just where the tubes connected to the globe. As the creatures on the platform scurried about, the image of their mysterious leader bellowing out its bellicose commands from within the vapor-filled orb, Tunuhun reached up with his free hand and lit the flare at the top of the package that he'd attached to the shaft of his weapon. With a brilliant flash of sizzling flame, the flare burst into life, its light betraying our position as it bathed us both in a sputtering, reddish glow. Without waiting for the creatures below us to react, Tunuhun reared back his arm and hurled the spear with all of his not inconsiderable might.

Just like he'd been aiming at the hump of a whale from the prow of an *umiak,* his accuracy was inescapable. The spear, although somewhat wobbly in flight from the added weight of the incendiary device, shot through the air straight on target, penetrating the strange apparatus just where the tubes met with the globe to send up a shower of red and blue sparks as the flare continued its sulfurous blaze. The creatures screeched and whistled upon seeing this and many of them, their convoluted, ellipsoid-shaped heads now writhing with tentacular rage, turned unerringly toward us where we stood in the shadows on the gantries above them.

For a few brief moments, the tableau held, the makeshift flare fuse burning its way toward the chemical and gun-powder payload as the beings below us whistled and hooted their displeasure. I couldn't breathe, couldn't tear my eyes away from the spear as smoke began to pour forth from the end of the device, the flames now taking on a greenish tint as they interacted with the chemicals Tunuhun had mixed together from our meager supplies. I found that I was gripping the bulbous railing so tight that the substance beneath my clenched hands cracked from the pressure, fluids leaking out to coat my fingers in a foul-smelling stench. As I continued to stare at the blazing spear tip, reciting silent prayers to our ancestors, the flames sputtered, fizzled, and then died out with a final, meager puff of unimpressive, yellow ochre fumes.

We had failed.

Below us, the creatures burst into a flurry of activity. From out of an aperture in the wall, they began taking peculiar, hand-held artifacts that appeared to be weapons, the first example I'd seen thus far of them actually arming themselves. Within the globe, the hideous monstrosity yammered out in disharmonious discord, issuing what sounded like a string of orders in its own laborious language. Amidst this cacophony of commands, the beings below us continued to grab the diabolical devices out of the storage locker until it was empty. Then, with a swiftness that made me blanch in pure, unadulterated terror, they streamed from the platform in waves, the warriors spreading their huge, dragonfly-like wings to take flight, while the smaller ones scurried off into the tunnels, most likely to come at us through the room we'd so recently vacated. With my frenzied heart beating like a trapped bird within my chest and ice water flowing through my veins, I turned to Tunuhun, intent upon fleeing this place of unimaginable horrors as quickly as possible.

Only to find that he was no longer there.

His constant disappearances were becoming insufferable, the more so as I realized that there would be no chance of rescue this time around. Nothing he could do at this point would possibly save me from painful evisceration or the certainty of a long, cold trip through space as a disembodied mind trapped within a brain cylinder. Even though it was clear to me now that there was no way in which I could survive such an all-out attack by so many beings armed with such advanced technology, I wished him well, hoping that his own escape might facilitate a military strike on this hellish base in the very near future.

Standing on the overhead gantry holding my wholly inadequate spear in trembling hands, I watched on in stunned silence as a veritable cloud of warrior creatures flew toward me, weapons held ready in their pincer-like foreclaws. It was nothing less than my own doom approaching, accompanied by the sounds of outraged lesser insectoids who were nearing my position through the surrounding tunnels of this age-old vault of alien madness.

-8-

I only had seconds to decide my next course of action. The huge, armored swarm of eldritch nightmares bristling now with weapons of an advanced and unfamiliar design, swirled upward from the platform below in a cloud of flapping, multilegged malevolence while from behind me there came the ever–increasing cacophony of hundreds of claw tips scratching and scraping their way through the gloom of the access tunnel.

My mind whirled with emotions, the clamoring of the adrenalized fervor of the fight-or-flight response spurring me to action. Around me I saw that the honeycombed cells of the hibernation units now Flickered to life at an ever-increasing rate, the pods and the occupants within them seeming to throb as they were awoken by the garbled yammering coming from the image of their unholy overlord floating within the glowing sphere.

I was in trouble, and that was an understatement to be sure. Scanning the surrounding area, I tried to locate a way out or find anything that would give me some small chance of survival. The walkway I stood on receded into the darkness in either direction, the gantries running all the way around the circumference of the mountain's interior as far as I could see. I noted with a desperate flash of hope that there were several other apertures spaced along the walls, perhaps other entries into rooms like the one from which we'd fled earlier.

As I prepared to make a run for the closest of these alternate tunnels, a sound like the hum of a microwave oven accompanied by the short, staccato burst of a machine-shop air gun ricocheted around me, warning me to duck out of the way. Just beyond me, a fracture appeared in the wall, lines zigzagging out from it in a spider web pattern like the cracks in a rock-dinged windshield. Sparing a brief glance back in the direction it came from, I saw that the flying horde had begun to fire their unusual weapons at me. Some type of sound wave device I surmised as I ran like a madman for the cover of the nearest hexagonal exit that did not have scuttling claws clackering along its darkened depths.

I had almost reached this possible escape route, shots peppering the walls around me, when a group of the smaller creatures burst forth from the tunnel through which I'd come earlier. I wondered if Tunuhun had fled in that direction or if he had instead taken one of these other corridors when he'd abandoned me here to die. That thought perhaps did him an injustice, but there it was. Already, I had begun to resent the fact that I was now going to be taken by these creatures, most likely to suffer the same fate as Opeim or something far worse since I'd interfered with their infernal machines. I supposed there was nothing to be done for it now.

Raising my spear in the manner in which I'd been taught by my elders from a very young age, I prepared to sell my life as dearly as possible. The advancing creatures had seen me now and came at me all at once, swarming over the gantries like an odious intrusion of overgrown cockroaches.

Then, from behind me, I heard the sudden flapping of ponderous wings and turned in time to thrust my spear into the chest of the first flying warrior that crested the railing. Grasping at my spear and hissing in anger, the creature spiraled neatly over my head, seeking to take the weapon with it, or perhaps just trying to minimize the damage I'd inflicted.

Using this to my advantage, I pivoted my hips. Keeping a firm grip on the weapon as it sailed over me, I then used the creature's forward momentum to swing it crashing down into the oncoming mob of its smaller brethren. Whether it was luck or just skill returning to me from all those years of whaling, I had made a very palpable hit; the sharp end of my spear had sunk into a joint where the forearm joined its thorax. As purplish ichor spurted out, it thrashed, yanking the spear from my hands and then taking most of the smaller creatures with it as they all sailed over the edge of the gantry in a tangled, writhing ball. My victory was short-lived, however, as hundreds more of the vile things poured out from the other apertures to join those now soaring above me on great, membranous wings. Here, deep within the heart of their secret base after sleeping for perhaps hundreds of thousands of years, they reigned supreme – there was nothing further I could do to stop them.

Unable to withstand the horror of what was going on around me, my mind fractured, my sanity fleeing in a mass exodus that left me bereft of all reason and incapable of forming coherent thoughts. Overcome by a fit of incongruous giggling, I fell to the floor, heaving and roiling with an internal amusement beyond my control. The last sane thought I had was to wonder why I was laughing so hard before I succumbed fully to the fit. Rolling and clutching at my sides, I sank into gibbering madness as the infuriated insectoids mobbed me, their writhing, multiple head tentacles glowing eerily in the pulsating illumination of the gigantic globe floating just below us all.

As they clutched at me with their claw-tipped appendages, something within my fear-addled brain suddenly clicked and I found myself awash in an alien consciousness. My anxiety and madness were taken from me and I felt that I was floating, tiny and insignificant, trapped within my own mind while this other persona took control. It was a vast intelligence and so beyond my understanding that I cringed within myself, attempting to make the bits of me that were still aware even smaller, to remain as still and as quiet as possible so as not to attract the attention of this gargantuan presence within me. Without conscious direction, my mouth opened and a string of inhuman phrases issued forth, a complex set of babbled warnings and instructions that I had no way of deciphering.

But these nonsense elucidations had a direct impact upon my attackers as the swarm fell still, communicating with one another in a high-pitched buzzing as their cranial tentacles wove in intricate patterns, cycling through a spectrum of colors I could no longer identify.

Deep inside me, my own tiny thoughts whirled with questions. The intellect overlaid atop my own was beyond my comprehension, yet somehow familiar, and I racked my brain trying to figure out what the connection was. Then it struck me. I'd felt that same presence when I'd been touched by the creature who'd been strapped to the table within the room of torture. The pictographs I'd seen carved upon the slabs we'd found coupled with the things Opeim had told us and the mental images I'd experienced upon contact with that hellish prisoner, all of it suddenly snapped into clearer focus within my mind causing me to experience a stunning epiphany.

These ancient races of star-traveling lifeforms had been enemies for uncountable ages. Throughout space and time, they'd fought and struggled against one another, battling across innumerous worlds hidden in the darkest depths of uncharted space. As I shared thoughts with the creature now in control of me, I saw vistas open before my mind's eye, the knowledge of an advanced civilization expanding within me, showing me things I was never meant to behold. I realized that, for whatever reason, the starheaded, barrel-bodied prisoner was trying to help me, perhaps in an attempt to foil its own sworn enemies.

Yet once again, its thoughts were too much for me to assimilate and so I flailed, pushing back against the scenes of untold wonder and ultimate horror which unraveled within my fragile intellect. The human mind was not evolved enough to hold such knowledge and still remain unchanged by it. So, I rejected the intrusion, shoving the creature's unwanted presence deep into my subconscious as I struggled to rise above it all and regain control of myself once more.

The whole experience took mere seconds as the creatures around me buzzed and clicked, undoubtedly discussing what would ultimately seal my inconsequential fate. With a final, mighty effort, I extricated myself from the invading persona and found that I was once more in command of my own thoughts. What I would do now besides die a horrible death with my disembodied mind packed up and carried out into the stars within a brain canister,

I did not know, but at least I would perish without being some star-spawned creature's puppet.

The multilegged, knobby-skinned insectoids still clutched at me, their writhing cranial tentacles displaying a range of colors that now seemed to be in concert with one another. Realizing I had no further chances of survival, my mind once again reeled toward madness. As my eyes darted about seeking any means of escape yet seeing only the looming presence of the repellent fiends surrounding me on all sides, I began to hear a strange and unfamiliar call.

It was a low cry, but one that nonetheless permeated the very air around us. Its vibrant, moaning cadence not unlike a Gregorian chant shuddered forth in a long, drawn-out intonation that seemed to come from more than one voice, as if there was a hellish choir situated somewhere far back within the walls of this facility. Its effect on the creatures surrounding me was instantaneous.

As one, they jerked erect, the tentacles sprouting from the convoluted, sponge-like surface of their craniums twisting about, the colors there now flashing in crimson hues. Without a backward glance, they left me, the warriors launching themselves from the gantry in droves, their wings beating the air with fluttering rapidity, while the others scuttled en masse for the nearest exits along the catwalk.

I was shocked and grateful by this unexpected reprieve, yet terrified all the same. That moaning vocalization had set the hairs on my arms to standing on end; even my human mind could easily identify the haunting call as a greater threat than the creatures who'd held me just moments before. Gathering my courage, I climbed to my feet, leaning on the railing for support, and then peered over the side to see what was going on.

The scene below me was chaos. The great being within the sphere howled in angry reproach as its minions flew and scuttled about it like ants swarming around the queen of their colony. I still could not bear to look full upon the image of the foul creature encased within that pulsating, indigo globe, so averted my eyes to study the patterns forming and reforming within the ranks of its servants now flocking to it from all sides.

Above the sphere, more and more of the warriors emerged from the sleeping cells lining the walls, their bulky, articulated limbs drawing them from age-old slumber as they clambered out of the hexagonal pods and stretched their wings for the first time in what must have been many thousands of years. As for the smaller creatures, there was an even greater multitude of them now, pouring out onto the open space below me from several of the connecting tunnels surrounding the platform itself.

Then I began to see the effects of what I'd done in the room with the strange machinery. The glow from the sphere below me decreased in intensity as I watched the creatures continue to congregate around it, but the light from the celestine pillars at the very bottom of the mountain's central shaft increased proportionately, its pulsating emissions becoming brighter than I'd noted before. I may have interrupted their communications network, but the power gathering within the rest of the mountainous base was undiminished. I realized with a sinking heart that the awakening would continue, perhaps even portending the beginning of a hostile invasion the rest of humanity was unprepared to deal with.

Gnashing my teeth in frustration, I wondered if there was anything more I could do to prevent them from reaching the surface of our world while simultaneously accepting how hopeless my situation had become. I was going to die here. And there was no way to stop these creatures from spreading across our entire planet once they'd completed their reanimation cycle.

The low, drawn-out moaning sounded again, this time much closer than it had been before, and icy chills ran up and down my spine as the reverberations of that haunting call filled the air around me. Something was coming. I didn't know exactly what it was, but the creatures who swarmed below me seemed ill-prepared to deal with it. Studying their movements, I remained rooted to the spot by fear and uncertainty as I debated my fate. Did I die here alone, trapped upon this gantry until I was overcome by whichever of these insectoid creatures first remembered my presence? Or did I run back into the tunnels, straight into the arms of whatever fiendish horror now awaited me there?

Alone, bereft of weapons, and over-matched by everything around me, I stood frozen by maddening indecision, sure of only one thing—my own imminent demise.

-9-

My waffling indecisiveness was interrupted by sounds I'd been hearing for some time, but were only now beginning to register within the current chaos of my troubled mind. Like a distant series of humming pops, the noises intensified as they came closer to my position, an ever-increasing *rar-a-tat-tat* of displaced air accompanied by explosive electrical reverberations. It struck me in one of my rare moments of total lucidity that the creatures who had built this place were fighting something far back within the tunnels. It was the discharge of their strange weapons that I'd been hearing over the groaning baritone of that fearful moaning, and I leaned over the gantry railing to get a better look into the darkened depths of that central corridor from whence it came.

Below me the semi-organized chaos of this nest of ancient, interstellar lifeforms began to sort itself into recognizable patterns, egged on by the vocal extortions of the monstrous being floating inside of the flickering globe. I noted with some small satisfaction that the sphere shimmered with far less illumination than before, even though I still could not bear to let my eyes linger upon its hideous occupant without risking the loss of even more of my slipping sanity. Whatever my sabotage of their infernal machines had done, it was having quite an effect. I only hoped that I'd interrupted the signal long enough to shut down their outgoing message in time. It didn't seem likely given the fact that there was a hellish, nightmare-inducing face peering out from within the sphere and issuing orders even now. Still, I did have some hope that a message sent from Earth would take light-years to reach the sector of space from which these beings had originated.

Yet the globe itself and its unknown occupant were a technological conundrum I no longer had time to puzzle about. Whether or not it was tied to their communications system was swiftly becoming irrelevant when compared to my own continuing survival. Right now, I needed to get ahold of myself and focus on escaping before it was too late.

To that effect, I bent all of my remaining intellect to the problem at hand, studying the patterns the insectoids were forming with single-minded determination. Geometric shapes seemed to be one of the reoccurring themes within their society and so it was even now while readying themselves for battle. Forming pentagons with the central point of each configuration resting closest to their leader, the creatures gathered into interlocking units, their multiple appendages latching together at the shoulder joints while their foremost limbs aimed the strange weapons that had been collected from storage vaults along the walls. It was like a huge colony of ants building a structure from their own bodies out of sheer necessity, yet with these creatures, it had a quite definite purpose. It was clear to me that they'd formed these tactical groupings on many previous occasions since they now executed them with near lockstep precision. Within moments, they'd collected themselves into several of these interconnected pentagons, bristling with weapons pointed unerringly at the main corridor leading back into the depths of the mountain fortress.

Glancing up, I studied the ever-increasing number of flying warriors above me and saw that they swarmed in distinct patterns of their own, the insubstantiality of their multiphasic bodies looping together and gyrating at incredible speeds. It was hypnotic to watch and I dropped my eyes from that unnerving sight lest I lose myself in its compelling, gyrational allure.

All of this gathering together into formations took place while the sounds of battle drifted ever-closer and I couldn't help but wonder what the devil was going on back in those twisted tunnels. Then, with a jolt of cold realization, I imagined that I already knew what it could be, a supposition that struck me as so utterly terrifying that I slid to the floor of the suspended walkway, clutching at the railings while my eyes were dragged inexorably back to the central corridor once more.

In desperation, I racked my brain for any other explanation, denying the very thought of what I felt could be the only thing that would possibly pose a threat to these creatures within their own unassailable hive.

Then, like a nightmare sprung to life from my deepest, darkest dreams, the central tunnel suddenly seethed with movement as several of the insectoid creatures were ejected back out of it to land in a broken heap in front of their pentagon-forming brethren. Something within the shadowy interior of that foul thoroughfare was thrusting its way forward, seeking to come forth into the pale, diminishing glow of the failing sphere, something too awful to even contemplate.

The pentagons the creatures had formed began to twirl like pinwheels, the weapons of each row of creatures discharging in turn, spatting forth a never-ending barrage of sonic projectiles as the warriors flying above whirled faster and faster, releasing some type of cosmic artillery that disappeared into the opening to seek out the enemy hidden within. The resulting cacophony of explosive energy released as they struck, accompanied by the staccato discharges of smaller weapons fire, was deafening and created a billowing dust cloud where the archway had once been. After a few moments, the gargantuan presence within the globe bellowed out a guttural command and the barrage ceased. As the dust began to clear and the sphere's illumination dimmed even further, I strained my eyes to see what stirred within that shrouded corridor, hoping against hope that my fearful suspicions would prove to be incorrect.

A moment can seem like an eternity when your mind has been pushed to the brink of madness and so it seemed to me as I sat staring with mounting anxiety at the bombardment-mottled hole that the settling debris slowly revealed. I could not tear my eyes from it, not even to check and see what the whirling, gyrating clusters of flying warriors above me were doing. The moment stretched, the tension building until I could stand it no longer. Rising to my feet, I leaned far out over the railing again, clutching at it with sweat-slicked hands, my eyes squinting in a vain attempt to penetrate the throbbing, all-consuming blackness that swirled and eddied just inside the tunnel's gaping mouth.

There was movement there, subtle at first, then blooming into a swifter motion that I could scarcely track with the naked eye. As I watched on, my insides quaking and my body twitching with psychogenetic shivers, rubbery, ill-formed appendages snaked forward from that shadowy corridor, latching onto the edges of the partially-destroyed archway. Into the relative silence that had reigned since the insectoid creatures had ceased their fire, there then arose a chilling vocalization that warbled through the hollowness of the mountain's central cavern, groaning its way into a keening intonation that shook the very air around me. The vibrations of that haunting call went straight down to the bone. No longer able to stand, I sank to my knees again in the chilling darkness while the pentagons once more began their mad, circuitous attack accompanied by the aerial bombardment of the multiphasic swarms above me. Amidst this rising swell of ear-splitting explosions came further sounds that issued forth from all the other entrances surrounding the globe platform, like the amplified mewlings of a thousand feral cats yowling in disharmonious agony.

Shuddering in uncontrollable terror, I watched as the quivering cluster of tentacles gripping the outer edges of the tunnel mouth thickened and then melded together to cover the entire rim of the huge portal in a writhing, membranous gasket. The concentrated attack that was still being directed against it was withering – I knew that no army of man could have withstood such a brutal barrage. But whatever was coming down that tunnel just shrugged it off, the thickening tissues clutching at the sides of the opening suddenly bunching up to pull the rest of the amorphous, blob-like entity forward in an oozing, repellent mass. Within the fading light of the flickering blue sphere, the entirety of it was thus revealed in all of its nightmarish glory.

My horrified suspicions had proven correct; it was the genetically-engineered servant of the barrel-shaped prisoners which had somehow been set free from its holding tank.

Having only the vague, repressed memories of my shared mental moments with the star-headed being to go off of, I didn't know for certain what this thing was capable of. But I did know with a sudden unnatural clarity that these fluidic, ever-changing lifeforms were created for the sole purpose of heavy labor and as such their power was staggering. Like an oversized amoeba, it formed a never-ending variety of limbs, claws, and other less identifiable appendages at the ends of its groping pseudopods, slapping the insect creatures out of its way like a small child knocking aside toy army men. It was madness incarnate and as I watched, spellbound by its voracious attack, it flowed across the middle of the platform and then enveloped the glowing globe within its massive, gelatinous body.

The response of the surviving insectoids was fearsome to behold. They swarmed over the protoplasmic blob like a plague of locusts, hundreds of the smaller creatures attempting to overwhelm it by sheer numbers while the larger, flying warriors dove at it from all sides. There was a sudden dimming of the lights within the mountainous cavity before the power surged back to full capacity. I could only assume that my attempt at sabotage had somehow been negated.

From within the creature's membranous body, the globe suddenly shimmered with a renewed radiance, its bruised and battered fluctuations permeating the darkness with a ghastly violet glow as the light leaked through the layers of quivering pink flesh now surrounding it. And over the horrendous noise of the battle, there still came the ever-increasing cacophony of mewling cries from the other apertures surrounding the central platform. My head swiveled back and forth, watching in amazement as these tunnels suddenly filled with several hundred of the star-headed, barrel-shaped beings who'd once been held captive in silent, unintentional sleep for as long as this subterranean base had been sealed beneath miles of ice and tundra.

When I'd been inside that terrible chamber back in the corridor beyond the control room, I'd taken great pains not to put too much effort into studying these beings. The tenuous hold I had upon my own sanity, especially after my unwilling communion with the prisoner who'd been strapped to the table, had dissuaded me from taking too close a look at them before we vacated that hellish place. It was a decision made at a time of great stress while fighting to retain my independence from the insidious mental manipulations of the captive creature, thus preventing the total madness that had nearly incapacitated me. Now I simply stared, unable to tear my eyes away from the abhorrent spectacle of their multitudinous arrival.

Each of them was perhaps six feet in height and shaped like a plump ferocactus with bulging ridges running vertically from top to bottom. Situated at the base of their rotund bodies was an appendage shaped like a starfish with elongated arms. These expanding and contracting digits served as locomotion, allowing the creatures to scuttle forward with an agility that was not unlike the rapid pace of a giant sea spider. At the very top of their barrel-shaped anatomy rested what can only be described as the head, another star-shaped extremity with eyes and mouths located at the very tips of each separate point. In addition to these physical characteristics, other tentacles radiated from around their midsections, and these branching, cilia-tipped limbs now held unfamiliar devices of a configuration that I'd never before seen.

How they'd escaped and just where they'd gotten these outlandish accouterments, I had no idea. All I knew for sure was that they were attacking their sworn enemies now with a vicious ferocity, perhaps in a last-ditch effort to regain their freedom after such a prolonged period of enforced captivity. Within me, alien thoughts and images stirred, struggling to rise to the surface again in what I took to be an attempt at communication, but I shut them out, holding onto my slipping sanity with the fading strength of all my remaining willpower. I wanted no more of their insufferable meddling inside of my mind; I'd had enough of it for now. So I shoved it down deep, locking it away within my subconscious until I could feel it no more.

The sounds of battle raging beneath my precarious perch drew my attention back from these unwanted intrusions into my scattered thoughts just as a series of sharp cracks and pinging noises rang out above the commotion. Glancing down, I saw the last of the cables and pylons holding the great globe in place break apart. Then the whole mass of it teetered for a few brief moments before it tilted into the open shaft, carrying the amoeba-like minion and a great deal of the attacking swarm along with it as it plummeted from the platform. While I watched in silent astonishment, the glowing sphere, enfolded by layers of the horrific creature's rubbery, translucent flesh and trailing hundreds of the smaller insectoids, spun end-over-end, spiraling down toward the power crystals located at the very bottom of the mountain's central cavity. I realized then it would be only moments before it struck and I had no idea what to expect when it did, but with a surety that came from somewhere deep within me, I knew that the consequences would be dire indeed. As the barrel-shaped beings began to fire their own weapons into the multitudes of remaining insect creatures, I searched for a way out, some way I could save myself from whatever was about to happen next. And that's when I heard it.

It was the clear, whistling call of a green-winged teal.

Peering around for the source of that incongruous bird song, my heart surged with new hope. It was the signal we'd used while hunting and one I'd been familiar with all of my life. It struck me then that Tunuhun must have released these beings and their servant from the holding tanks back in that room of torture. My unflattering criticism of him earlier now proved to be entirely unfounded as I realized he hadn't abandoned me at all, but had instead done the only thing possible, the one thing that could perhaps prevent us both from suffering a fate far worse than death. A fate that our friend Opeim had already endured.

Scanning the darkness, I finally saw him crouching within one of the tunnel openings just a few feet away from where I now stood. I could not describe the sense of relief that flooded me while I stared at him, trembling in relief and grinning like an idiot as he motioned for me to follow him back into the waiting corridor.

But then an explosion shook the ancient base as the globe struck the celestine pillars and I collapsed to my knees on the wildly bucking walkway, holding on for dear life as clouds of smoke and flame shot upward from below. Glancing down while struggling to keep from falling off the writhing gantry, I saw that the destruction of the sphere had instigated a chain reaction of epic proportions. Another series of explosions rocked me then and I cried out in despair as the entire mountain began to crumble, the suspended structure I clung to twisting a final time before breaking apart beneath my trembling hands.

-10-

The suspended walkway rippled under my booted feet as it started to fall, soon to be joining huge pieces of the mountain's interior and chunks of honeycombed cells which were now plummeting toward the chaos reigning far below us. Bursting into action, I ran. But with a succession of Violent popping noises the gantry cables snapped as I flew past, the strands of the support wires Spurting dark fluids as they whipped around me like dozens of hissing, spitting snakes. With a final herculean effort, I leapt, the gantry twisting away beneath me as I sailed through the debris filled air with my hand stretched out toward Tunuhun.

But our fingertips brushed together without catching as I missed and slammed into the wall just below the tunnel entrance instead.

The incised stonework underneath the opening bit into my chest, driving the air from my lungs as I scrabbled at the lined and pitted surface in an attempt to find purchase. Yet my hands, frenzied from terror and trembling in reactive fear, were unable to close upon anything that could stop my fall. Clawing at the decorations covering the alien architecture, I started to plummet backward into the open air of the central shaft, beginning what was sure to be a drop of several thousand feet.

As gravity pulled me from the wall of the ancient base, beginning my plunge into the explosion-filled abyss below me, I was suddenly jerked to a stop, saved at the last second by nothing more than the hood of my parka. Holding firmly to this durable scrap of clothing, Tunuhun grunted with the strain of hauling me back up and over the edge. Then, hand over hand, he pulled me through the archway with all of the considerable power of his well-muscled physique. After dragging me deeper into the dubious safety of the quaking tunnel, he stumbled, collapsing as our bodies tangled together in a heap upon the floor of the unstable passageway.

Yet there was no time to catch our breath, and we struggled back to our feet, breaking apart from each other in what would have at any other time seemed like a ridiculous amount of hilarious fumbling. Then, without even a hint of shared levity, we took off down the shuddering hallway, fighting for balance while the floors and walls continued to buck and shake around us as we fled.

I didn't know where he thought we were heading; to my mind, escape now seemed like an impossible dream. But we kept on running, the will to survive driving us onward even if the outcome was far less than certain for the both of us. Soon the noises of the battle still raging behind us were quickly drowned out by the hideous, nausea-inducing grinding made by the mountain itself as it continued to deteriorate.

As I scrambled down that quaking corridor, I felt the questing thoughts of the barrel-shaped being again tickling at the corners of my mind, trying to break through and somehow reach back into my guarded thoughts, perhaps to divulge even more of its unfathomable knowledge. Refusing this insidious attempt at communication, I continued following Tunuhun through the crumbling tunnels, moving ever forward without any real knowledge of where he was leading us now or why.

This hive, this ancient bastion of a lost, space-faring race, was never meant to exist in our present day and age. Built in some long-ago era before the planet was even remotely habitable for humankind, it had become trapped by an unanticipated ice age. Afterward, its creators had remained here, caught in an unending sleep cycle, waiting for thousands upon thousands of years for a random seismic event to thrust their mountainous stronghold back up into the light of day once more.

And those other creatures that had been imprisoned here with them, that antediluvian race they'd been fighting with for uncountable eons, they'd once built bases here as well, judging by what I could glean from those pictographic slabs we'd found.

What other strange and hidden wonders did our planet yet contain, what incomprehensible installations like this one or primordial, ice-covered cities lost for hundreds of thousands of years did our world yet conceal? Much of Earth remains unexplored, from the polar ice caps to the depths of the oceans to the hearts of the steaming jungles. What else might we discover if only we knew where to look?

As I ran, I realized the beings within this mountain would surely threaten the continued survival of the entire human race. If these things could get a signal out to their place of origin, all of humanity would be in jeopardy. There was no way we would be able to stand against such advanced technology, against weapons and a species that was so far beyond us in both evolution and scientific development. If these creatures ever rose to the surface of our world, or if that behemoth of gelatinous death, that slave creation of those other barrel-shaped beings, somehow escaped destruction ... I shuddered to think of what would become of us all.

I decided right then and there that if we somehow survived, I would find a way to stop them, a way to save mankind from the depredations of these advanced, star-spawned beings of ancient and unknown origin.

But for the next few moments everything else became a blur. It was all happening too fast, the pressure behind my eyes building as I ran, the thoughts of the creature from that torture chamber pressing in at my mind from all sides, its desires only hinted at as it continued to attempt to invade my every thought.

Yet I could not let that happen.

Unprepared to deal with such an insidious attack, I tried to throw up defenses, like shimmering barriers of thought within my mind. But time and time again each one was torn asunder by the mental assault of that unrelenting creature. Stumbling, I fell to my knees in the shuddering darkness, clutching my pounding head, fingers grasping at fistfuls of sweat-soaked hair as my facial features scrunched up in unbearable pain. Unable to withstand the strain of it any longer, I became insensate, sliding willfully into the beckoning arms of deepest oblivion.

* * *

When I came swimming back up into consciousness, waking from odd dreams of cyclopean cities and eldritch artifacts of arcane yet unfamiliar function, I found myself lying within an enclosed space, sweat rolling off me like I was resting inside of a blast furnace. Struggling for breath in the hot, fetid air, I opened my eyes, glancing around in groggy bewilderment. Above me was a quadruple pane of clear, glass-like substance set into angles to form a rectangular prism. With a jolt of panic, I realized I was inside one of the specimen tanks from the torture room. The transparent surface of the device was clouded over with condensation, but I could see light leaking in from outside. On the verge of panic, I began to thrash about, raising my fists to pound against the enclosure holding me captive, a capsule that was perhaps even now transporting me to some alien world located in a galaxy far from Earth.

"Pai-qasuaq."

Tunuhun's voice stopped me from my adrenaline-fueled struggling, telling me in his own quiet way to remain calm. Then I felt him move around behind me, one of his arms held across my chest as he sought to extricate himself from beneath my flailing limbs. After he managed to reposition his body next to mine, he lifted his free hand and tapped at the side of the unit we were encased in, cracking it open at a hidden seam he'd somehow figured out how to manipulate while releasing its previous occupants. The transparent cover above me pivoted outward to reveal the deteriorating mountain base, but from quite a distance away. It was still sinking into the earth, fires and explosions raging unchecked as it collapsed back in upon itself. Sitting up, I gathered together the tatters of my shredded courage and then began to take stock of our situation.

The holding tank we were lying in rested in a long divot plowed across the tundra in one of the small meadows that dotted the landscape of this mountainous region. There were many other pits and gouges marring the surrounding area as well which contained an assortment of jettisoned technology that turned the field into a graveyard of smoking hot, metallic debris. I was able to deduce from this that we'd been blasted clear during one of the explosions. How we'd gotten into the specimen tank to begin with was still a mystery to me, but I could guess with some degree of confidence that my friend had once again saved my life. The pressure behind my eyes was gone for now and so I took a moment to climb out of the tube and unbutton my parka in the heat-filled air.

The fires painted the arctic skies above us in vivid oranges and reds while huge clouds of smoke and fumes funneled up from the newly forming crater. It was not unlike the aftermath of a volcanic eruption, I decided. Tunuhun climbed out to stand beside me and now studied the mountain as it sank back into the ground, the grandeur of the Brooks Range providing a stunning backdrop as the ancient base continued its self-destruction. With the rampant rumbling and successive explosive concussions coming from within the still collapsing, subterranean cavity, I was surprised to hear other reverberations rising above us on the wind. Following the repetitive, choppy-sounding noise, I stared up into the darkening sky and watched as several helicopters, most of them military-issued Black Hawks, came into view and then began descending to the ground a little ways away from us. As they touched down, men wearing combat-ready hazmat suits poured out, while still other more heavily armed personnel began off-loading equipment in an incredibly efficient manner. *It's about time,* I thought, watching as three people split off from the main group and then began to approach us.

They were just about halfway to our position when the smallest of the three stepped in front of the one that I took to be their leader and stopped him with an upraised arm. Gesturing to us and then back to the men swarming around the grounded helicopters, he made several remarks unheard by us at this distance. After a moment of silent consideration, the leader nodded his consent and his associate spoke into a radio microphone that was attached to the shoulder of his hazmat suit. Four additional men then detached themselves from the group by the helicopters and came toward us at a run, pulling heavy machine guns of an unfamiliar design around from carrying straps as they did so. It appeared these soldiers were taking no chances and I could only speculate that it was because we were standing in front of a contraption that had come from within the deteriorating base itself. The armed men sprinted up to where we stood and then fanned out, while another member of the landing party left the main group by the helicopters to join the three still approaching us across the smoking, pitted ground of the small mountain meadow.

Once the soldiers had us covered, the additional man jogged forward, taking a small device from a pouch at his belt. Kneeling next to the specimen tank, he then began an investigation with the electronic, hand-held unit, concentrating as the device made a series of beeps and clicks while he passed it over the different parts of the open tube. Meanwhile, the three officers moved to stand just a few feet away, studying us with an intensity that I found to be bit unnerving. Beside me, Tunuhun grunted low in his throat, clearly not impressed.

I noticed then that these three all wore a modified version of the standard CBRN suit worn by the rest of their soldiers but designed to allow for a face-shielded helmet which connected to a more streamlined and fully armored outfit. The coloration of their modified protective clothing showcased shades of black instead of the more traditional camouflage worn by the other troops, and its configuration allowed for their insignia and weapon harnesses to be more strategically placed as well.

The man in the middle of the group stared at us from behind the helmet's clear face plate, his watery-blue eyes intense above a craggy yet clean-shaven countenance. To his left the larger soldier was your standard military type with a muscular build and the disapproving, flat-faced look of a beached halibut. I didn't like him right off the bat and decided to watch what I said around him from this point forward. Turning my attention to the smallest of the three officers, I was surprised to find a woman. She gazed at me with expressive green eyes, her steady, forthright manner visible in the way she held herself and in how she continued to take in all her surroundings, even as her superior focused solely upon us.

After staring at us for several long minutes, the man in charge glanced over at the technician still taking readings on the transport tank and then raised a bushy gray eyebrow. The man nodded his head, snapping his scanning device closed to return it to the pouch at his belt. Waving the tech away, the commander then strode forward to study us from just a couple of feet away.

"I'm Director Lionel Walker from the EDA," he said in a gruff voice. Then he gestured to his subordinates in turn, "and this is Deputy Director William Forsythe and Assistant Deputy Anna Wilkenson. We're here to seal off and contain this area while also finding out what exactly happened here. And you two gentlemen are going to help us."

"Director," Anna warned, stepping forward to place a rigid arm in front of him, "these men have been compromised. I strongly advise that we take them into custody and make sure they aren't a threat before you get any closer. We'll be able to question them further after verifying that it's safe, sir."

The director smiled indulgently, brushing her away with the casual disregard of a superior officer. "Really, Anna, do you truly think that these *Eskimos* are going to pose any real threat to us? They're unarmed and they look like they can barely stand on their own two feet as it is. We need to know what happened here. I want to find out what these men have seen and just where they've been in the last few hours."

"With all due respect, sir," she replied, "these men may have been influenced by forces we currently know next-to-nothing about. Until we've determined the full extent of their contamination, protocol demands that we process them as potentially hostile."

"What do you think, Will?" he asked, glancing over at his second-in-command.

William's cold, dead eyes bore into me, searching for what I could scarcely fathom. After a moment, he turned back to his superior. "I hate to admit it, sir, but she's right. We know nothing about these two men. I'd advise extreme caution until we've discovered more about what's going on around here."

Making a face like he'd just bitten into a sour lemon, the director conceded with ill-concealed contempt. "Very well," he muttered, turning to one of the soldiers who still had us targeted. "Take them into custody and make sure they get a full spectrum work up with Doc Brandywine. I want them ready for questioning as soon as possible, understood?"

"Yes, sir!" the man replied as the rest of his team closed in on us.

I felt Tunuhun tensing up at my side, so I flipped him a hand signal, letting him know to stand down. There was no way we could fight our way out of this situation and I didn't think I even wanted to try. I was tired. *Really* tired. I just wanted this to be over so we could get back to the village and warn the elders about what we'd seen here, begin doing what we could to ensure the safety of our tribe. My eyes drifted back to the smoking crater, my thoughts wondering just what remained alive at the bottom of that artificial shaft.

As if summoned by my thoughts alone, the earth suddenly heaved, the ground bucking underneath us as a thunderous explosion from the crater split the air. The men around us stumbled as they tried to retain their footing, calling out to each other in practiced, military fashion, too experienced to panic in the face of what, in their line of work, must have seemed almost like an everyday occurrence. But I knew what was coming; I could feel it in my mind as alien thoughts pressed against my consciousness once more, nearly driving me to my knees in shocked surprise.

About six feet to the left of us, glowing, celestite pillars trailing clods of dirt and ice thrust themselves up out of the tundra, followed by a large pylon that extruded from the mossy turf like a lumbering bear awakened from a seasonal slumber. What at first appeared as a solid, hexagonally-shaped wall at the front end of this strange formation dilated into a wide, open hatchway, and out of this maw of unutterable darkness flew a cloud of the warrior insectoids. Swarming like a colony of gigantic bats, they spiraled up into the smoke-filled sky followed by hundreds of the smaller creatures who then came pouring out of the bowels of the earth behind them.

The men around us burst into immediate action, unfazed by the appearance of so many unusual enemies. Grabbing the director by the arm, his female deputy pulled him toward the safety of a fortified base camp that had been established near the military helicopters, firing into the oncoming multitudes with her side arm as she went. As the elite soldiers formed into squads, attempting to stem the tide of assailants now attacking their front lines, I signaled to Tunuhun. We were getting the hell out of here – I wanted no part of the conflict that was raging on around us and I was bound and determined to vacate this entire area as soon as possible.

Searching our surroundings with that intent set firmly in my thoughts, I spied a helicopter resting a little ways behind us. It was not one of the many military types, instead being more of a standard freight hauler, but it would have to do. Breaking into a run, we left the pandemonium of the erupting battle behind, dodging and swerving around clumps of heavy, hand-to-claw fighting as we went.

It was a very near thing, but we were able to reach the chopper and throw open the passenger side door without being mobbed. The flying warriors now blackened the already darkening sky, while the smaller insectoids near the tunnel mouth formed into their battle pentagons, spitting out a brutal barrage of sonic annihilation that was taking a dramatic toll on the over-matched soldiers. The scene was utter chaos.

Climbing into the helicopter, I glanced at the surprised pilot. He was a civilian by the looks of it, wearing an old, beat-up flight jacket with a ratty fur collar and a sombrero hanging across his back that was being held in place by a chin strap secured around his throat. His eyes were hidden by aviator sunglasses, but as he saw us getting in, his lips twisted into a sardonic smile from inside of a thick, bushy beard.

"We need to get out of here," I told him in no uncertain terms. "Right now."

Running a hand back through his long, wavy brown hair, he blew out a puff of air through pursed lips before flicking switches in preparation for takeoff. "Those bastards commandeered my bird as I was getting ready to do a supply run," he stated matter-of-factly, "so I don't owe them a goddamn thing. Strap yourselves in – It's going to be a bumpy ride."

I buckled into the copilot seat as Tunuhun scrambled over me to tumble into the back, settling into another seat in the cargo area. As the helicopter lifted off, the pilot maneuvered around the swarming warrior creatures, but they took little notice of us as they were too busy engaging with the ground troops below. Our liftoff was dicey for the first few minutes as we slammed into a few of them during our ascent, but then we were clear of the gyrating, multiphasic bodies and began climbing to an even greater altitude.

My thoughts were a jumble of conflicting emotions. Even though I knew there was nothing we could do to help the men on the ground, the guilt of leaving them there to fight on alone consumed me. I comforted myself with the knowledge that we could've been detained and questioned for hours, perhaps even days. I was unfamiliar with the EDA and not even sure of what the acronym stood for. For all I knew, they could have taken us to some hidden government facility where no one would have ever learned what I'd discovered, and then nobody I cared about would have been able to prepare for what I saw coming. We needed to be free in order to do what was needed to stop this madness. For that was what I planned to do with my hard-earned knowledge; I would stop these creatures by any means necessary from taking over the planet.

I just didn't know how best to go about it yet.

The pressure of the alien thoughts lessened now that we were underway, but I knew I would never be free from their pervasive influence. They indicated to me that the lifeform I'd communed with was still alive and for some reason, I could also sense that it had retreated far underground. I didn't know what awaited it there, but I got the impression that it had its own set of plans. Right now, I feared to open that door within my mind to discover anything more. I couldn't risk losing myself in an alien consciousness right now. For what I needed to do, I had to be able to think clearly.

Just where did we start with the defense of the planet? Was there anyone on Earth who could help us? Perhaps my aunt would know. My late uncle had been the one to finance all of my schooling upon her request. Old and eccentric, she was a rich widower now who'd had a lifetime of experience from her husband's strange obsession with researching the hidden mysteries of the world. As the wife of an archaeologist, she'd seen many things; undoubtedly, she must know a lot about what my uncle had uncovered during his travels. Maybe she could help, but that still left us without anything else to go on. Where did we begin this search for more information on these ancient creatures? What could we do to defend against them? And just how did we go about stopping them when the time came? I was lost in thought when I felt Tunuhun tap me on the shoulder.

Turning as far around as my seatbelt harness would allow, I glanced back at him to see what he wanted. He gazed at me, his face once more filled with the impassiveness I knew so well. It was reassuring that, without even asking, I knew in my heart I could count on him no matter what happened next.

Without breaking eye contact, he reached into the folds of the parka he still had tied around his waist, his muscles rippling beneath his sweated thermal in the shadows of the cargo compartment. Working his way around the belt straps that held him securely in place, he managed to retrieve a flat, semi-circular piece of broken stone about the size of my hand. Nodding to me, he then handed it over.

Taking it, I held it up to the fading light of the evening sky, studying it closely. It was a chunk of debris from the room we'd first fallen into during the earthquake the night before. Even though it was only a partial fragment, I could see that it was a piece of a larger pictograph, some sort of chart. The pressure within my mind suddenly increased as the alien thoughts pushed through my defenses. While I struggled to seal them off again in my subconscious, information leaked through, coloring my perceptions of the fragment with otherworldly understanding.

It was the beginnings of a map.

I was sure of it as I regained control of myself, thrusting the images back down with a shake of my head. We definitely had something worth looking

into here, something to work with. If only we could find other sites like the one below us, maybe we could piece together what this map tile was trying to tell me. It was a place to start at least. As I closed my fist around the carven stone, I held onto the conviction that we would succeed. We had to for the sake of the planet and the future of all mankind.

"Where to, pal?" the pilot shouted over the whir of the blades. "I don't mean to be a downer, but I have to get back and take care of my deliveries. We don't have enough fuel left to just fly around up here all night. But, damn! Am I gonna have one hellova story to tell the guys back at the shop! What the fuck were those things anyway?"

I didn't know what they were any more than he did. But there was one thing crystal clear in my mind:

I would find out and I would stop them.

About the Author

William H. Nelson is the author of Nathrotep (2018) and Within the Range of Reanimation (2020). He grew up in Anchorage, Alaska where he attended college at UAA. During his time there, he was a regular contributor to several publications, including The  Radical (Radical Publications, 1992-94), The Auroran (Denali Publications 1993-96), and Rainsongs (Denali Publications 1995-96).

After moving to the Seattle area in 1998, he met the love of his life, Lisa, and now lives with her and their cat Dipso, named from the Greek word meaning 'thirsty'. William continues to write every day. In his spare time, he enjoys reading voraciously, playing the drums like a berserk spider-monkey, creating award-winning costumes and props for local conventions, watching movies with a passion bordering on obsession, and playing selections from his truly ginormous collection of epic fantasy board games.

Connect with William on Facebook!
www.facebook.com/williamhnelsonbooks

www.ingramcontent.com/pod-product-compliance
Lightning Source LLC
Chambersburg PA
CBHW071532100726
47908CB00004B/1367